EXPOSED--TRIBUTE BRIDES OF THE DREXIAN WARRIORS #3

TANA STONE

Broadmoor Books

Chapter One

Zayn worked the chains fastened around his wrists, feeling the weak spot he'd made over the past few weeks with a loose shard of steel. Just a little more and he'd be free, he thought, straining against the metal and pushing the pain aside. Blood trickled down his wrist, but he ignored the sharp tang that hit his nose. It wasn't worse than anything else he'd smelled since being thrown into the dungeon over a month ago.

He glanced around the dank cell that held nothing more than a cot and a metal bucket. Considering how technologically advanced his enemy was, Zayn had been surprised to find their prison so rudimentary. Of course, he hadn't known just how advanced the Kronock had become until he'd been taken captive.

He let out a low growl, and the rusted metal walls echoed it back to him. Being captured had not been part of the plan. As a member of the Drexian military team sent to infiltrate a research colony near enemy space, his mission had been to defeat the Kronock and gather intelligence on their research. That hadn't worked out so well when his entire team had been slaughtered by an enemy considerably more sophisticated than they'd suspected. Well, not the entire team. Him, they'd kept alive.

1

He tried not to think about the surprise attack that had left the other warriors dead and had landed him inside a Kronock prison. His people hadn't ventured into enemy territory in decades, battling their crude and brutish foes on the borders of Kronock space and repelling the would-be invaders on the outskirts of the solar system the Drexians protected. They had no need. The Kronock were predictable in their attacks, but they were outmatched by Drexian technology and warfare. Had been since they first attempted to invade Earth over thirty years earlier. Or so his people had thought.

Zayn's blood heated as he flashed back to how easily the Kronock had disabled their weapons, the efficient way the gray-scaled creatures had slaughtered his comrades, and the sophisticated ship they'd dragged him onto, bloody and broken. It was clear to him now that the enemy had spent years lying low and pretending to be oafish brutes, all the while developing technology to blow the Drexians—and Earthlings—out of the sky.

The only thing they hadn't changed was how they tortured captives. That had been old school. A sharp pain pierced his side as he breathed in too quickly, and he knew he had at least one broken rib. The skin on his arms had stopped healing from the lashes he'd taken with a laser whip, the gashes deep and oozing. He shook off the discomfort. They would heal once he was away from the daily abuse, as would the flesh on his wrist he was scraping off as he loosened his chains. The crucial thing was getting off the ship and back to his people so he could tell them what he'd learned.

Zayn tugged at his wrists and felt the metal give, finally snapping and clattering to the floor. He paused to listen for the rush of feet, but there was nothing. He touched his raw flesh, grateful to be free of the shackles and the burden of dragging the heavy chain with him when he moved. Shaking his hands to regain some of the feeling, he ran them through his hair. It had become shaggy and matted in the weeks or months he'd been held—he'd lost all track of time in the dank cell—and his fingers tangled in the dark locks.

"Time to have another chat with the General," a voice said, from the end of the corridor.

His auditory implant made it easy for him to understand the guttural words of his enemy, but still, the rough sounds grated on his nerves.

Zayn reluctantly picked up the chains again and held them around his wrists, flinching from the contact and hoping his jailor wouldn't notice the broken clasp. He didn't respond to the Kronock. He never did. He never said a word, a tactic that had earned him more electric shocks than he could count, and beatings so severe he usually blacked out and had to be carried back to his cell. The worst had been when they'd electrified the bumpy nodes running along the length of his spine. Normally an indicator of arousal, they were sensitive to touch, and he'd writhed in pain each time they'd sent a jolt through them.

A tall alien approached the door, his wide, clawed feet tapping on the floor and announcing his arrival before his bald, scaled head appeared in the window. He looked at Zayn through the metal panel grafted to his eye socket, and the red, bionic eye flashed as it scanned him. Zayn had learned that aside from being huge and strong, some of the Kronock had augmented themselves with technology, the bionic eyes being the most obvious addition. He knew there was more he couldn't see beneath the armor grafted to their scales, which was why they'd been able to overpower him and his team. Zayn swallowed the taste of bile as he thought of how outmatched they'd been. That was why he would need to be faster and smarter to make it out alive.

As the door creaked open, Zayn took a breath. *This is it*, he thought. *Now or never.*

The Kronock stepped inside to take him by the arm as he usually did, but at the last moment Zayn feinted to one side, rolling his shoulder and spinning around, before whipping the chains around the jailor's head and darting for the door. Stunned, it took the Kronock a moment to react, and by that time, Zayn had slammed the door shut behind him and locked him in.

Zayn didn't stop to listen for the roar of frustration. He was already halfway down the corridor, when he heard a noise to his left and swung his head toward one of the cell doors. The noise wasn't the harsh language of the Kronock. It was the Drexian language. It might have been weeks or months since he'd heard it spoken anywhere but in his own head, but he knew the sound of his own tongue.

He glanced through the window cut into the door and saw a bare, muscular back hunched over in the corner, the bronze skin and raised nodes confirming his initial guess. This was a Drexian.

"Brother," he called out. "Come with me."

The man raised his head but didn't turn. "You're Drexian?"

"Yes," Zayn said, impatient to get away but not willing to leave another warrior behind. "I'm getting out of here, and you're coming with me."

The Drexian shook his head. "Impossible. Go without me."

"I can get you out," Zayn said, leaning against the metal door and stumbling forward when it swung open easily.

The Drexian prisoner stood, his hands in tight fights by his side. "It's too late for me. Go before they come for you."

Zayn started to shake his head when the other prisoner turned and focused his red, bionic eye on him. "They've made me one of them. I can't go back after what they've done to me. After what they've put inside my head." His arms shook as he spoke. "Even now, I have an urge to kill you."

Grek. Zayn backed away, his throat constricting and making it difficult to speak.

"Go," the Drexian hybrid strode forward and pushed the door shut. "Save yourself."

Zayn stumbled away, his eyes not leaving the unlocked cell door.

"Wait," the Drexian called after him.

Zayn met his gaze through the window in the door.

"The next time you see me." The red eye blinked as he spoke. "Do not hesitate to kill me."

Zayn didn't answer, his gut twisting in a knot as he continued down the hall. The guard station was empty, but the metal wall cabinet that held extra weapons was not, although it was locked. He ripped the cabinet door off its hinges and grabbed two blasters from inside. He guessed he had no more than a minute before his escape was detected, so he needed to move fast. He pushed the thought of the other Drexian warrior out of his mind. If he let the feelings of rage and regret fill him, he would not be able to do what he needed to do.

Running down another narrow hallway, Zayn ducked into a closet as he heard footsteps pounding toward him. He'd learned what he knew about the ship by feigning unconsciousness when he was dragged back and forth from being tortured. Sometimes his eyes really had been swollen shut, but other times he'd only pretended to be half dead. If his memory served him, the shuttle bays and flight decks were one level up. He glanced above him, breathing a sigh of relief when he saw a vent covering.

Zayn clambered up into the ceiling and pulled the covering back into place. Crawling as quietly as he could, he followed the vents up, using his elbows and knees to gain traction in the tubes. When he was sure he'd reached the right level, he slid a panel back and dipped his head down.

The corridor was empty, so he lowered himself, holding on with one hand as he slid the ceiling panel back into place before landing on the floor with a thud. He kept close to the wall as he hurried toward a wide door, which slid open as soon as he stood in front of it.

"You're going to make it," he whispered to himself as he took in the expansive flight deck.

Ducking out of sight behind a stack of metal containers, he eyed the array of ships. He needed to find one that was leaving as soon as possible, and one big enough on which to stow away. That eliminated the shiny, two-seater fighters, and the cargo ships still loading up. His gaze lingered on a rusted, banged-up ship, and he watched a squat alien pilot stride on board.

"A scavenger," he said, rubbing his hands together. He recognized the short, purple-skinned alien as a trader of space junk. It wasn't the fastest ship, or the best smelling, but it would probably get the least amount of scrutiny.

Edging his way around the flight deck by darting between crates and containers, he dashed up the ship's ramp as it began to lift and rolled inside. As he watched the ramp slam shut behind him, he flinched. After being the only member of his team to survive, he was now leaving a Drexian behind. Not really a Drexian anymore, he reminded himself, taking a breath and trying not to think of the metal eye implant grafted into his kinsman's flesh.

He looked around the quiet ship and guessed the captain was busy piloting, so he crept to the rear, slipping into a particularly dirty bathroom just big enough for him to close the door while holding his breath.

Zayn felt the ship begin to move, then accelerate, and when he felt the jump to light speed he let his shoulders relax long enough to shift the grip on his blaster. He stepped out and cracked his neck by twisting it from side to side. "Time to talk to the pilot about setting a new course."

Chapter Two

K atie walked along Rodeo Drive, her camera tucked into a pink leather bag slung over her shoulder as she scouted the sidewalk looking for celebrities. She tried to act casual as she peered into the storefronts, but she was a bundle of nerves. It didn't help that it was a thousand degrees, and she'd had to cover her hair with a scarf.

"Come on," she muttered to herself. "There has to be a Hilton heiress out shopping today. Or a Kardashian. I *need* something."

A thin woman carrying a beige Birkin bag gave her a sideways glance. Katie sized her up as no one worth photographing and gave her what she hoped was her most innocent smile. The woman wasn't fooled and moved away, shooting a nasty look over her shoulder.

This was a disaster. She knew her desperation was palpable, which was the kiss of death in her business. Even though she was tall, with striking curly, red hair and more curves than were typically accepted in LA, she'd always had the confidence to blend in anywhere. It probably came from growing up with a father who was a grifter and had taught her everything from three card Monte to how to work a mark. It wasn't tough to see that he was why she'd ended up as a paparazzo for some of the top Internet gossip sites.

"I just need one shot," she said, more to bolster her confidence than anything. "Just one great shot to get me through this."

This meant the disaster that had become her life since she'd taken the last known photo of the socialite Mandy Talbot before she disappeared. Katie closed her eyes briefly, willing herself to go back in time and *not* take that image of Mandy outside of the restaurant after her best friend and TV starlet London had left their standing lunch date.

At the time, Katie had thought it was gold. Mandy was clearly distraught in the image, and the headline the tabloid rag ran next to it proclaimed the TV producer's daughter to be an "Instagram diva ditched by best friend and boyfriend." It had netted Katie a tidy sum, enough to cover rent, since her stand-up-comedian boyfriend hadn't gotten a gig in weeks. It had also been the last image anyone could find of the woman who had apparently vanished the day the photo was taken.

Katie had been interviewed by the police, and by the private investigators hired by Mandy's dad. Somehow, those investigators had been able to dig into her financial life and see the debt she was in. That was all they needed to decide she was somehow involved in the disappearance, and it had all been downhill from there. She'd ended up on the pages of the very magazines she usually shot for, headlines proclaiming her as the last person to see the heiress alive and painting a picture of her as someone with nothing to lose.

She adjusted her oversized sunglasses. Part of her was glad her father hadn't lived to see this. She was supposed to be the one hunting for celebrities trying to blend in or avoid detection, not the one hiding. Not that she'd been shocked when her fellow paparazzi had turned on her. No honor among thieves, and all that.

"Katie!" A voice from across the street made her jump and turn before she could stop herself. She heard the click of a shutter.

She cursed at herself. "Shit, Katie, you know better."

She started walking briskly in the other direction, dodging people and trying to put distance between herself and the photographer. She thought it might be that weasely guy from the *Enquirer*, but no way was she going to turn around to check. Figures, she thought. Only the bottom feeders were still hounding her after all these weeks.

"Where's Mandy?" the voice yelled after her.

At this point, people were staring and beginning to recognize her. She kept her head down and held her bag tight, barely avoiding a run-in with one of the Schwarzenegger kids. Damn, she should have been taking his photo, not trying to avoid flattening him while she made a run for it.

She ducked around the corner and nearly ran the two blocks to where she'd parked her piece-of-shit car. Jumping in, she tossed her bag on the passenger seat and floored it, looking in the rearview mirror once she was moving. No one behind her, that was good. But she hadn't gotten a single photo. That was bad.

It took her almost an hour to reach her apartment in the Valley, which gave Katie plenty of time to think about just how badly her life was falling apart, since her car's radio wasn't working.

"Think," she told herself, letting the wind from the open window cool her. "What would dad do?"

He'd managed to get himself out of plenty of scrapes over the years, and he'd usually been guilty as hell. How had she managed to get herself in such a big mess without having done anything wrong?

The problem was Mandy's TV producer dad and his rabid dog

investigators. They seemed hell-bent on blaming the girl's disappearance on someone, and didn't seem to be too concerned about the details. Katie had thought the dad was faking it the first time he'd appeared on the news with his collagen-enhanced third wife. She knew a faker when she saw one, and that guy didn't give a shit about finding his daughter. He wanted people to think he did, though. Hence the private investigators eager to find a fall guy.

Katie pulled up in front of her apartment building and the car shuddered to a stop. She rubbed her fingers on the steering wheel and whispered to the car, "I just need you to hold out a little bit longer. I really can't take one more thing going wrong right now."

What she needed was to provide an ironclad alibi to the police and have them call off the investigators. And the best way to do that was to enlist the help of her boyfriend. He may not be great when it came to making money, but she knew he had her back when it mattered. At least she thought he did.

Katie took the stairs to her third-floor, garden apartment two at a time, waving at an elderly neighbor, who clearly didn't read tabloid news since she smiled brightly. She opened her front door and called out as she walked inside.

"Mark, I need your help—" The words died on her lips as she stood in the near-empty living room, looking at a faded couch and an empty TV stand.

The flat screen was gone, along with the contents of the bookshelf and the framed prints on the wall, leaving metal hooks to dangle at eye level. Her mouth went dry and she dropped her bag and keys on the floor.

No, this wasn't happening. It couldn't be happening. How had they been robbed? Mark was supposed to be home all day.

"Mark?" She went into the bedroom, and saw that her laptop was gone from her desk. She opened the closet and her heart tightened.

Where her boyfriend's clothes had been were only a few wire hangers, but her clothes were all still there. They hadn't been robbed. Mark had left. "And that bastard took my computer."

She pulled her cell phone from her pocket and dialed his number as she stomped back into the living room. She didn't mind his leaving, nearly as much as she minded him taking everything of value in the apartment. The asshole hadn't even paid for any of it.

Katie instinctively went into the kitchen and flipped open the box on the counter from Dot & Dough. He'd even eaten the last of her custard-filled doughnuts. It was official. If she ever found him, she was going to kill him.

Her call went straight to voicemail, as she tossed the empty doughnut box in the trash and returned to the living room. Typical. She doubted he'd be answering any of her calls from now on. She left him a colorful message telling him exactly what she thought of him, then threw the phone onto the carpeted floor, sinking down next to it and letting her head fall into her hands. She was broke, and she'd been cleaned out, and her stomach was growling from hunger.

After a moment, she straightened up. Mark had been right, even if she hated him for being the first one to think of it. She had to get out of there. She didn't have money for rent, and that was due in less than a week. She couldn't make money with every paparazzi in town angling for a photo of her. She needed to get out of town before it was too late.

She hurried back to the bedroom, reaching under the bed for her suitcase. Nothing. The dick had even taken her suitcase.

"You have got to be shitting me," she screamed, then took a deep breath and tried to shake it off. It was fine. She'd just have to pile her clothes onto the back seat of her car.

She grabbed an armful of shirts from the closet and headed for the front door, stopping and nearly dropping them when she saw the man standing in the doorway. If she wasn't already so upset, alarm bells would have been going off in the back of her head. As it was, she was too irritated to be afraid, even though the man had to be almost seven feet tall and built like a linebacker.

"Can I help you?"

He wore sunglasses so she couldn't see his eyes, but he pivoted his head to take in the shabby surroundings. "I believe it will be the other way around."

Chapter Three

Zayn flexed his shoulder muscles and hit the punching bag again. It felt good to be able to move his arms. The doctors on the station had told him his rib was completely healed, but he flinched as he pulled his arm back again. He may be healed, but he could still feel the ache of the muscles that had been bruised so badly. He welcomed the pain, though. His atonement for surviving the mission no one else had.

A bead of sweat trickled down his forehead, and he swiped it from his eyes. It had been a long time since he'd been in a gym this well equipped. He looked around at the wide room, with the high ceiling and punching bags hovering in mid air. Mats covered part of the floor, and there were several weight benches and sophisticated training machines in one corner. A shirtless Drexian warrior dodged punches thrown by a holographic opponent in a ring that levitated several feet off the floor, and another threw javelins at shimmering holographic targets spiraling through the air above.

Zayn had heard that the station—know as the Boat—was the best equipped in the Drexian Empire, but he'd never seen it for himself. He also knew the opulence had been created for the tribute brides who were brought to be mated with the Drexian warriors. He'd only seen a small portion of the station so far, but what he'd seen had impressed him.

He knew that much of the elaborate environments relied on holographic technology to create oceans, mountains, and exotic deserts, but even the other areas were impressive. The officers' lounge had a stunning view of space, and the main open-air atrium soared over twenty stories in the air with a clear domed ceiling. For a soldier who'd been kept in a dimly lit cell for weeks, everything on the gleaming station seemed a little too bright and a bit forced. Part of him wished there had been a closer Drexian outpost or ship, but the Drexian ship that intercepted him had brought him here. He doubted the scavenger whose ship he'd hijacked would have been happy to fly all the way to the Drexian home world, although the Jerengi scavenger had been well compensated for his detour—even if Zayn had used his blaster to do most of the convincing.

Zayn crushed his fist against the punching bag and grunted from the impact. It felt strange to be somewhere dedicated to pleasure and seduction. Neither of those had ever been high on his list of skills. Sure, he visited some of the pleasure planets with his fellow warriors, but he'd never felt comfortable on them or with the various alien females that had been paraded in front of him.

Even the name of the station sounded strange to him. Casually referred to as the Boat, it was actually dubbed The Love Boat—a reference to something on Earth that the station's designers used for inspiration. He couldn't imagine why humans would have a floating vessel for love, but he found the idea of humans strange, in general.

Physically smaller than his species, not to mention technologically inferior, humans were systematically destroying their own planet, yet focused few resources on discovering places to migrate to off-world. He'd heard the Earthlings weren't even aware of the existence of alien species, which he found laughable. If they weren't genetically compatible, he knew the Drexians never would have made first contact or established the mating agreement.

Unfortunately, Drexians no longer produced females, so it had been necessary to find a compatible species. Luckily, humans had been a match and they had also been a target of the Kronock. His species stepped in with an offer to defend Earth from invasion if Earth would provide a select number of females for Drexian warriors to take as mates. The governments on Earth had agreed, as long as the deal was secret and the general population never knew. That had been thirty years ago.

Zayn had a hard time reconciling life as a Drexian warrior with romancing Earth females. The few he'd seen aboard the station looked too soft and delicate for someone like him to touch. He hit the punching bag again, and droplets of sweat fell from his brow.

The door at the far end opened, and a man entered in formal military uniform. Most of the Drexians he'd seen on the station were in casual clothes or, at the most, fatigues. He recognized the officer as one of the ones who'd debriefed him after his arrival. Kax, that was his name. Kax of House Baraat. One of the ruling families, not a commoner like him.

"Looking good," Kax said, approaching him with his hands clasped behind his back. The dark uniform of the Drexian military looked pristine with a highly decorated sash across one shoulder.

Zayn steadied the punching bag and raised a wrapped hand to his chest in salute.

"I hear your wounds are healing well."

"Yes, sir," Zayn said. "The medical team here is excellent."

Kax grinned. "I think you may have met my brother's mate in the medical bay."

"The human?" Zayn remembered a pretty female with long,

brown hair who'd cleaned his wounds. She'd talked a lot, but hadn't looked at him like the damaged soldier he was, and he'd been grateful for that. "I remember her."

Kax shifted from one leg to the other. "She's still training."

"Do all tribute brides have tasks?" Zayn caught another rivulet of sweat with a wrapped hand before it went into his eye.

Kax shook his head. "No, but we try to keep them happy, so if they want to work, we encourage it. My own mate is teaching other tributes dance."

Zayn cocked an eyebrow, but didn't ask why tribute brides needed to dance. "A few more days, and I should be cleared to return to duty. At least, according to the doctors."

Kax cleared his throat. "The High Command doesn't want to send you back out again so soon. Not after what you've been through. You brought us valuable intelligence. Information we can use in our fight against the Kronock. That deserves a reward, don't you think?"

"No reward necessary," Zayn said, almost flinching at the thought of receiving praise for his failed mission. "Just doing my duty."

"Well, you're getting a reward anyway," Kax said. "At least, High Command thinks it's a reward."

Zayn rested his hands on his waist and tilted his head to one side.

Kax slapped him on the shoulder. "Don't look so terrified. You've been matched."

"Matched?"

Kax glanced around him. "You do know where you are, don't you?"

Zayn followed his gaze around the gym.

Kax laughed. "A tribute bride. You've been matched with a tribute bride from Earth."

Zayn's stomach tightened. "I thought they'd stopped the transports until the situation with the Kronock is settled."

Kax shrugged. "Apparently this one was a special favor for my sister-in-law."

What did that mean, Zayn wondered. Why was his tribute bride a special favor?

Kax must have noticed his confused expression. "My sister-in-law can be very persuasive. That's probably all I should say."

"But I never requested a tribute bride," Zayn said, the nervous churn in his stomach persisting. "I never submitted an application."

"Well, they couldn't exactly send you back out on another mission so soon. And I can't think of anyone more deserving."

Zayn watched the fellow officer's eyes move around the room and wondered what he wasn't saying. He'd had enough training to know when someone was keeping something from him, and there was definitely more to this than Zayn was being told. Did they want an excuse to keep him on the station and under observation? He knew he couldn't ask point-blank, so he nodded. "Thank you, sir."

"My own honeymoon is almost over," Kax said. "I'm about to be deployed, and the intelligence you brought back should be very helpful."

Zayn looked the man up and down again, taking in his fancy uniform. "Deployed?"

"I'm returning to field work. Military intelligence." He rolled his shoulders back. "I've missed it sitting on the High Command. Now that we have new information on our enemy and their intentions, intelligence gathering is more important than ever."

Zayn felt a pang of guilt that this was the man who would be following up on his information. It should be him going back out there. He was the one who failed his team. He was the one who should take the risk, but he knew it was pointless to debate with his superiors.

"Good hunting, sir," Zayn said.

"Thanks." Kax said, his mouth quirking up slightly.

As Kax turned away, Zayn grabbed his sleeve. "Wait. There's something I didn't mention before."

"Go on."

"The other prisoner in the cells? He was Drexian."

"You said you were the only survivor."

"I was, and I didn't know anyone else was being held until I was escaping."

Kax crossed his arms. "You couldn't get him out with you?"

Zayn heard the judgment in the question and felt shame flood his face. "He wouldn't come."

Kax waited for him to continue.

Zayn closed his eyes for a moment. "I've been second-guessing myself, telling myself that I was seeing things, telling myself that he wasn't real. They tortured me so much I could've been hallucinating."

"But you don't think you were, do you?"

"No," Zayn said, letting the word rush out of him. "The other prisoner was Drexian, at least he used to be Drexian. He was also part machine." His voice broke. "The Kronock were turning him into one of them. He had an eye implant, and said they'd been putting things in his head. He said he was fighting an urge to kill me."

The muscles in Kax's jaw twitched. "I'll do some digging. Find out which of our warriors might have been taken by the Kronock. Some of our officers are on deep-cover assignments, so we may not know immediately."

"I wanted to get him out," Zayn said. "Even if he'd been brainwashed, it felt wrong leaving him."

"You did what you could." Kax gave him a curt nod. "Now finish up your workout, soldier, and go meet your bride."

Zayn watched Kax walk away and looked down at his bare arms. Even after healing, his forearms still had the puckered marks where the Kronock's laser whips had burned his flesh. He swallowed a sour taste in his mouth as he attempted to push the memory of his torture out of his mind, and he turned his focus back to the punching bag. What female would want a warrior who'd failed to protect those under him? If he couldn't save them, what kind of warrior was he? Not one who deserved a reward. What was the High Command really doing, matching him with an Earthling? Did they suspect the enemy had turned him? Were they using a tribute bride to distract him, or maybe to spy on him?

He slammed his fist into the bag and felt a satisfying jolt of pain. He knew one thing for sure. He would find out.

Chapter Four

Katie blinked a few times and stared up at the ceiling, the gossamer fabric draped above her billowing in the breeze. The air felt nice, better than the usual stifling LA heat. Had she left a window open in her bedroom?

She rubbed her eyes, wondering why her head felt so heavy, and rolled over on her side. Pushing herself up into a sitting position, she gaped at her luxurious surroundings. This was definitely not her bedroom. Was she having some sort of hallucination, or had she been air-dropped into an Abercrombie & Kent brochure?

Sweeping aside the sheer fabric that hung down around the bed, she gazed across the wide room that was open on three sides. The ceiling appeared to be buff-colored tent fabric, with dark, wood posts holding it high, and brushed-copper pendant lights dangling from several points. The floor was also dark wood, the wide beams gleaming in the late-afternoon sun. A jute rug covered part of the floor, and was topped with a rustic, leather trunk that had been repurposed as a coffee table. Past the large bedroom was a balcony overlooking an expansive savannah, with long grass and flat-topped trees in the distance.

Katie put a hand to her head, her feeling of grogginess now combined with confusion. Had she been sent on an assignment to Africa? Was she trailing some celebrities on vacation? Or maybe the British royal family? She knew they loved to visit Africa. But why didn't she remember anything?

The last thing she remembered was coming home and finding all of her stuff gone. She felt a flash of anger at the thought of her jerk boyfriend. Make that ex-boyfriend. So how did she end up halfway across the world, with no memory of getting there?

She glanced to her left, where a ceiling fan with leaf-shaped blades stirred the air lazily over a sitting area with a faded Persian carpet and a side table that held an old-fashioned typewriter. Was it possible she'd time traveled?

Don't be ridiculous, she told herself, scooting to the edge of the bed and moving the sheer fabric out of her way. *There's no such thing as time travel.*

She stood and took a moment to get her bearings. One thing she knew for sure, this was not LA. Not even the most elaborate movie sets were this convincing, she thought as she watched a herd of zebra amble past the balcony. As she moved toward them, she noticed a man sitting in one of the lounge chairs. She hadn't noticed him before, because her view had been blocked by a group of tall, potted palms clustered around one of the tent poles.

Her pulse quickened when he sat up and turned around, and she sucked in a sharp breath when she saw the scars on his muscled arms. They weren't fresh, but the obvious burn marks drew her eyes and almost distracted her from the sheer size of him.

She took a step back, even though he'd made no move toward her. He must have been six-and-a-half-feet tall. Or maybe seven. "Who are you?"

"Zayn," he said, as if that was a decent explanation for what he was doing in her room. At least, she assumed it was her room. Maybe she was in his room. She was going to go with her first assumption.

"Okay, Zayn," she said. "What are you doing in my room?"

He raked a hand through his dark, choppy hair, and the movement made his shirt ride up and expose a hard row of muscles on his stomach.

Holy crap, Katie thought watching his veined bicep strain against his dark green T-shirt. This guy was built.

"I'm sorry about this," he said. "It wasn't my idea. Not that you aren't very appealing."

She wasn't quite sure what to make of that answer. He didn't meet her gaze, but he also didn't seem dangerous, even as big as he was. Katie considered herself a pretty good judge of people after all the training her father given her. This guy might be big enough to snap her in half, but she got the definite sense that was the last thing he wanted to do. As a matter of fact, he looked like he was afraid of her.

"If it makes you feel any better," he said, "I'll probably be assigned another mission soon."

Mission? What was this guy talking about? Was it possible he was a photographer, too? Another paparazzo following her? She eyed him and tried to calm her rapid breathing. He didn't look like any photographer she'd ever seen.

"Do you have any idea where we are?" Katie asked.

"We're on the Boat," Zayn said. "From what I understand, this is the Safari wing."

Katie gave a small shake of her head. "Nothing you said just made any sense."

He looked up to meet her eyes, and Katie felt the air leave her. His eyes were a shade of blue she'd never seen before—like the brightest Caribbean water she could imagine. He locked eyes with her without saying a thing, and Katie realized she was holding her breath. There was pain in his expression, and it made her want to pull him into her arms, although she knew that was absurd. She still had no idea why this guy was in her room, or what boat he was talking about.

At that moment, the door burst open, and a slim woman with long, brown hair rushed in, followed by a woman at least a foot taller, with blue hair, and a short man who reminded Katie of a small ringmaster in his fuchsia suit. They were all talking at once, and the blue-haired lady was fluttering her hands.

"I'm so sorry we're late," the brown-haired woman said. "We were supposed to be here when you woke up."

"To ease the transition," the blue-haired lady said, holding out a hand. "I'm Reina, your liaison." She glanced over at Zayn and smiled. "I see you two have already met."

"Not really," Katie said. "I still don't know where I am, or what he's doing here."

"Well, isn't this perfect?" the short man said. "I told you, we should've taken her to the director."

"No way," Brown Hair said. "When I met the director, she freaked me out. I told you, this way would be better."

"I still prefer the game show," Reina said. "It was much more festive."

Brown Hair rolled her eyes. "It was archaic."

"She doesn't know?" Zayn closed the distance between them in a few long strides.

"Know what?" Katie asked, feeling her confusion quickly being replaced with impatience. "Are you all with a magazine or a website?"

"Don't be silly," the colorfully dressed man said. "I'm Serge, your wedding planner."

"I'm sorry, what?" Katie looked from face to face, but none of them broke into a laugh as if it was a joke.

"I still say the game show did it better," mumbled Reina.

"Why do I need a wedding planner?" Katie asked. "My boyfriend just dumped me and stole all my stuff. I think you've got the wrong girl."

"Your name is Katie Bishop, right?" The woman with long hair asked, glancing down at a tablet and scrolling across with one finger.

"Yes," Katie said. "But I think I'd know if I was engaged."

"You'd think, wouldn't you?" Serge drawled, as he looked her up and down and began to circle her.

Katie looked back at the woman with the tablet and something clicked in the back of her brain. "You're Mandy Talbot." She snapped her fingers and pointed. "You disappeared." She put her hands on her hips and glared at Mandy. "You're the reason my life is ruined."

Mandy smiled at her. "I know. That's why I insisted they bring you up here. I knew you'd be the perfect tribute bride. It sure beats staying on Earth and being framed for my disappearance, am I right?"

"Tribute what?" Katie asked, bewildered. "And what does that mean, 'staying on Earth'?"

"A tribute bride for the Drexian warriors," Mandy replied. "Let me explain. See, it all started about thirty years ago when Earth was about to be invaded by these really bad aliens called the Kronock. Disgusting creatures and nothing like the Drexians, who are also aliens but are extremely hot, FYI. The Drexians made a deal to protect us, and in return, Earth agreed to give them women to marry." She put a hand on Katie's arm and leaned in. "The Drexians ran out of women, or couldn't produce more, or something. So ever since then, they've been bringing Earth women up to this space station called the Boat for their warriors to marry."

Katie stared at her. "So what you're telling me is you went insane and ran off, right? And now you've kidnapped me, and concocted a crazy plot with these…" She waved a hand in the air. "People."

Mandy laughed. "I know it's a lot to take in. I felt the same way you did, at first. As a matter of fact, I was a lot less pleasant than you are. The long and short of it is that once you're picked to be a tribute bride, there's no going back. Can you imagine the chaos that would be caused if women returned to Earth and told everyone about the aliens who wanted to invade us, and the big, gorgeous aliens who are protecting us?"

"So you're telling me I'm one of these tribute brides?" Katie asked.

"That's right." Reina clapped her hands together. "You are matched with him." She pointed to Zayn, who'd walked to the edge of the balcony and was leaning on the wooden railing. "Isn't it exciting?"

Zayn turned around and looked at her again, his brows pressed together. Unless she'd lost her touch reading people, he wasn't any happier about this than she was.

Without a word, he walked past her and out of the suite. Well, there was her answer.

Chapter Five

Zayn stomped along the wooden pathway leading away from the suite. They hadn't told her. Hadn't explained anything to her. It was clear the human had no desire to take a mate. Much less him.

He fisted his hands by his side. She was too pretty and delicate anyway, with her smooth skin and soft curves. And he'd never seen hair the color of flame before. Her wondered what the mass of curls felt like, and imagined running his fingers through them, then gave his head a rough shake. She wouldn't want his callused hands touching her, and she definitely wouldn't want to be matched with someone like him. A disgraced warrior.

Not to mention, she'd already complained about being walked out on by another man. Zayn knew that as a soldier the chances he'd have to do the same were pretty high. He'd have to leave her to go on missions, and there was always a chance he wouldn't return. He hated the thought of abandoning anyone, or being responsible for anyone else's loss. He knew loss, understood loss, and would not be the reason for this female to experience any more of it.

He took the inclinator to the top floor, and found his way to the officers' club. He'd been in the warriors-only bar a few times during his short stay on the station, but it never ceased to impress him. Unlike most of the station, which was bright and white with lots of breathtaking, holographic vistas, this bar relied on nothing but a wide wall of high, curved windows looking out into space. Even though several warriors stood along the bar and others sat together at tables, the conversation was merely a low hum, interspersed with the sound of clinking glasses.

Zayn let his eyes adjust to the lower lighting and dark furniture, the only illumination coming from the artificial candles placed on each small, square table, and spaced down the length of the polished, black-lacquer bar. After being held in a dank cell, this club actually felt more comfortable to him than the wide skies and open-tented suite of the holographic environment he'd just come from. *The Safari Wing*, he reminded himself.

Zayn knew the space station had an entire division devoted to creating the holographic worlds for the tribute brides, but he'd never imagined something as elaborate as the one he'd been sent to. He assumed the environment was taken from a place on Earth, but he found it hard to imagine something as beautiful as that being real. The Drexian home world had been all but decimated generations ago, which was one of the reasons his people had taken to space and become such successful warriors. They'd learned to fight and defend themselves after their planet was ruined by invaders. Vowing never to lose anything again, the Drexians became known throughout the galaxy as fierce and fearless fighters.

Zayn considered himself one of these fearless warriors. Then why did he feel so afraid when he thought about taking a mate? He scraped a hand through his hair and gazed out the window.

"What's your poison?" the bartender called out.

Zayn turned and walked to the bar. Maybe a drink would help. He recognized the heavyset man with light-green skin as an Allurian;

one of the species the Drexians had saved from the Kronock. In his time aboard the station, he'd noticed a number of aliens from rescued civilizations.

"A Cressidian gin." Zayn allowed himself a small smile when the bartender pushed the glass of pale-pink liquid toward him. It had been a long time since he'd tasted good Cressidian gin. He took a drink and felt the burn all the way down to his stomach.

"You look like you've got the weight of the galaxy on your shoulders," the bartender said, as he wiped a cloth across the polished surface of the bar.

Zayn shrugged. "Nothing I can't handle."

The bartender nodded. "We get a lot of mated warriors here. The human females are attractive, but from what I hear, it isn't always easy."

"It's not that," Zayn said. "I've barely spoken two words to her, but I know I shouldn't be the one matched with her."

"Any reason why not?"

He thought it should be obvious. The bartender could see his scars and must have heard about the warrior who'd returned without the rest of his team. "I don't think I'd be good for anyone."

The bartender didn't respond.

"My last mission didn't go so well. I lost people. I was the only one to come back."

"Survivor's guilt?" The bartender poured more gin into his glass. "That doesn't mean you shouldn't be matched up."

"My job is dangerous," Zayn said. "There's a good chance I'd make this human a widow. It's not fair to her." He didn't say that it also wasn't a loss he was willing to risk. The sight of her had stirred protective urges in him, as well as desire, and that scared him.

"Not many Drexian warriors have desk jobs," the bartender said. "Taking a mate is always a risk."

Before Zayn could ask what an Allurian knew about human mates, the sound of loud footsteps caught his ears.

The short man in the wide-lapelled, fuchsia suit hurried toward him, stopping and putting his hands on his knees as he gasped for breath. "It would be much easier for me to plan these weddings if my brides and grooms would stop running off."

Zayn's mouth twitched up as he watched the man's cheeks flush bright-red from exertion. "Sorry about that. I didn't think she was interested in being a bride."

"Well, you're wrong."

Zayn's breath caught in his throat. "What do you mean? When I left she seemed pretty upset and confused."

The man straightened his lapels. "It only took a little bit of convincing for Katie to realize what an honor it is to be a tribute bride. I'm happy to say she's completely on board."

What had they said to convince the Earthling? She hadn't struck him as the type to go along with anything easily. "Are you sure?"

The question earned him a derisive snort. "Of course I'm sure. I'm taking her to select her wedding gown in the morning." He spun on one platform-heeled foot. "I trust you won't keep her up too late."

Zayn's cheeks stung. The thought of staying in the same room with the redheaded female made his mouth go dry and his cock swell. He was glad he stood in a dimly lit bar so no one could notice his arousal.

There was no way she wanted him, he thought, even if she'd agreed to the match. They must have given her a huge grekking incentive, and he wondered if it had anything to do with why he was matched in the first place. He didn't think she was in on it, but for all he knew, she could be an amazing actress. He'd been trained to sniff out deception, and he knew there was something off about a tribute bride being offered to him as soon as he returned from his failed mission and being held by the Kronock. And there was definitely something odd about a female changing her mind so quickly.

Even if she wasn't a spy, the thought of someone so pretty beside a scarred warrior like him didn't make sense. She deserved a Drexian who hadn't been tortured and marked by the enemy. One who hadn't been captured and disgraced. He couldn't reject the match, but he could resist the urge to mate with her, even though the thought of her made his pulse race. He couldn't allow his mind to be clouded by a female until he knew what part she played in this deception.

He inhaled deeply. He'd withstood the Kronock's torture. He could survive this. Zayn slammed back the rest of his gin and growled.

Chapter Six

"Again." Katie crossed her arms and tapped a foot on the floor.

Mandy sighed and signaled Reina, who entered a series of commands into her tablet. The African-safari setting disappeared, and they were left standing in a white-paneled dome, with only the basic furniture remaining. "Like I explained before. The fantasy suites are mostly holographic. Once you go out the door, you're in a holographic corridor that fits in with the setting and leads to other doors. Each suite is a self-contained holographic unit. There are six holographic wings on the station, and the rest of it is real."

Katie narrowed her eyes. "And it can be flipped on and off at will?"

Mandy nodded to Reina, and the savannah returned along, with the grazing gazelles. "I'm telling you. The Drexians have some pretty impressive technology." She winked. "As well as impressive other stuff."

Serge rolled his eyes, while Katie ignored Mandy's attempts to be buddy-buddy. She was still pissed that the socialite turned out to be perfectly fine, while Katie had been hounded by lawyers and press and accused of being behind the woman's disappearance.

She studied the former socialite for a moment. From all appearances, she was telling the truth. At least, she thought she was. As crazy as it sounded, the alien space station story would explain a lot. Like why Reina had gray skin and incredibly long limbs and fingers, and why Serge had abnormally large, round eyes and hair that seemed to change color at the roots when he got flustered or upset. She'd already seen it go from purple to pink and back again twice.

"If you're aliens, how can I understand you?" she asked Reina. "I know you can't all speak English."

Reina tapped a finger behind her ear. "A universal translator implant. They put it in when you were being transported from Earth, hon. You can understand what any alien says."

Katie touched a razor-thin scar behind her ear and swallowed hard, then looked at Mandy. "So, let's say I believe you. Are you telling me that you left Earth, got hitched to an alien, and are now planning to stay here? Forever?"

"You don't just 'get hitched,'" Serge said, putting a hand to his chest. "You get to have the wedding of your dreams. A wedding only the wealthiest Earthlings could afford."

"I'm not the kind of girl who grew up dreaming about being a bride," Katie said. She didn't say that she had grown up learning how to pick pockets and run long cons.

Serge frowned and muttered to himself, his roots going from purple to fuchsia once more.

Mandy sat down on the edge of the bed, pushing the sheer netting out of her way. "I know it sounds crazy, but I'm really happy here. I'm training to be a medic, which I could never do back in LA. Not with my family and reputation."

Reina beamed at Mandy. "She's come such a long way from those early temper tantrums."

Mandy blushed. "I didn't react as coolly as you are. I made a bit of a scene." She shrugged. "But then I fell in love with Dorn and made some friends. Not everyone stays on the Boat. Some go to one of the Drexian colonies, and I'm planning to join my mate on his battleship. It helps that my life on Earth was basically going nowhere." She tilted her head. "Are you sure my father's been looking for me?"

"So sure that I was on my way out of LA just to get away from his lawyer and PI goons. He's kept your disappearance in the news cycle for weeks."

Mandy's expression darkened. "Let me guess. He's appeared on TV with my stepmother? Made impassioned pleas for my safe return? Talked about how crushed he is to lose me?"

"Yeah, pretty much," Katie said. "How did you know?"

"Because my father is a publicity whore." Mandy sighed. "He doesn't care about me. Not really. He's using me to stay relevant."

"Well, he's been pretty convincing. I won't have anyone even pretending to miss me. No one will notice I'm gone except the old lady who lives below me and tells me to turn down my music." Katie blinked away tears, as she realized the truth in what she said.

Literally no one would even know she was gone. It wasn't like she had a regular job, or a boss to check in with. Her boyfriend was gone. She had almost no girlfriends, or close friends of any kind. You had to let people in to be friends, and Katie had learned never to get close to anyone, unless they were a mark. Her father had drummed that into her well.

Mandy stood and grabbed both of her hands. "See? You're the perfect tribute bride. None of us have close family or friends, and most of us are running from something—debt, bad boyfriends, cops."

Katie raised an eyebrow. "Is this a mating service or a penal colony?"

Mandy laughed. "That's a good one. You're funny."

Katie pulled away. "This holographic stuff is cool, but who's to say we aren't in some lab in Silicon Valley? This could all be some tech weirdo's wet dream to get women in here so he and his dorky friends can pretend to be aliens looking for mates."

Reina made a disapproving noise in the back of her throat, and Serge sucked in air so quickly Katie thought he might keel over.

"Did you see the warrior they'd paired you with?" Mandy asked. "Did Zayn look like a Silicon Valley geek to you?"

Katie had to admit that he hadn't. Actually, he might have been the hottest guy she'd ever seen in real life, which was saying something considering the number of celebrities she'd chased down. She thought of his dark hair and shockingly blue eyes, not to mention how big and built he was. No, Mandy was right. He was no basement-dwelling computer dork. "I mean, no, but that doesn't mean he's from another species, either."

"That's because you didn't see him without a shirt on," Mandy said, grinning. "Drexians have bumps from the back of their neck all the way down their spine that heat up and harden when they get turned on."

Serge made a few clucking noises, and Katie noticed Reina's pale-gray cheeks become a patchwork of pink splotches. Suddenly, the idea of Zayn getting aroused made her own body warm. She hated how much she suddenly wanted to see the bumps down his spine. And touch them.

"Oh, for heaven's sake." Serge stomped over and took her by the hand. "Come with me."

Even though he was half her size, Katie had to hurry along behind him to keep up as he barreled out of the suite and down the walkway. When they reached the end of the wooden path that arched past an open-air bar, Serge waved a hand over a flat panel and a door swished open. The corridor they entered look completely different from the area they'd left. Sleek and modern, with curved, white walls, the hallway looked every bit like it had been lifted from the pages of a futuristic novel. Serge paused at another door, and Mandy and Reina caught up with them.

"Do you mind if I ask where we're going?" Katie said.

Serge didn't look at her, and didn't release her hand. "You'll see."

The door opened, and he led them onto what appeared to be an elevator, waving his hand over another panel before the doors closed and they surged upward. Katie put her hand out for balance, as it seemed to swivel and continue at a slight angle as the lavender uplighting in the compartment pulsed.

"These elevators have a kick to them," she said.

"They're inclinators," Mandy told her, "because they don't just go up and down."

When the doors opened again, she followed Serge out, but now she couldn't help but gape. In front of her was an open-air pedestrian space, complete with cobbled streets and trees in planters. A fountain sat in the middle, with a stone cherub spraying water below him, and the glass-fronted shops would have looked at home in Beverly Hills. But it wasn't what was in front of her that made her stare. It was what was above.

The atrium had to be twenty stories high, with a clear ceiling that looked out onto an inky sky. A nearby moon made Katie do a double take, and then another one, when she realized it wasn't

Earth's moon. The elevator shaft she'd ridden in ran to the top, and spokes shot off it in various directions.

"Holy crap," she whispered. "What moon is that?"

"It's one of Saturn's," Reina said. "Isn't it beautiful?"

Katie's mouth was dry, but she managed to make a small noise.

"You aren't going to freak out and start hyperventilating, are you?" Mandy asked.

She shook her head. Even if she felt like it, she wouldn't give anyone the satisfaction. If this Hollywood princess could take it all in stride, so could she. "The Drex…"

"Drexians," Mandy finished for her.

"Right. Drexians," she said. "So the Drexians built all this just for the…"

"Tribute brides," Reina said. "Not at first, but they found there was less resistance to the idea when they packaged the concept more attractively. It took years to construct the space station and fit it out for humans. We had to adjust the gravity and develop a day and night cycle, since there isn't a sunrise or sunset out here."

Katie pulled her eyes from the view of space and focused on the people walking through the atrium. Earth women hand-in-hand with big, gorgeous men. Aliens who looked like Reina hurrying beside solo women. A handful of huge guys in badass military uniforms. A few men Serge's height, one walking what appeared to be a lemon-yellow puff of fur on a leash. If this was a con, it was the best one she'd ever seen. Her father would have loved this, and would have viewed space as the final frontier…for him to exploit. She wished he could see it.

A thought took hold in the back of her mind. What if she could let everyone on Earth see what she was seeing? A story like this would do more than save her career. It would make her rich. Any publication would pay a king's ransom for something this juicy. All she had to do was go along with whatever they had planned for her for a while, and compile evidence along the way. Then, when the time was right, she'd manage to sneak off the station—they had to go back to Earth for more women, right?—and drop a bombshell about the aliens, the women they were taking, and the tricked-out space station floating somewhere near Saturn.

"Do you need more convincing?" Mandy asked, putting an arm around her shoulders.

Reina handed her what looked like an ice cream cone topped with a lemon-yellow scoop. "Iced binjie. You'll love it. The other tributes say it tastes like frozen popcorn."

As she held the cone and tried not to cringe at the idea of frozen popcorn, Katie thought about the Drexian with the brilliant-blue eyes and the corded stomach, and her own stomach did a somersault. She didn't like the idea of tricking him—using marks had always been the part of the con she hated the most, and part of the reason she'd gotten out of the business—but if she wanted to get back to Earth and get back her life, she'd have to convince him along with everyone else. A hot guy like him would find someone else with no problem, she told herself. It's not like they even knew each other, after all.

She plastered on her most sincere smile, the one her father had made her practice in the mirror for hours on end. "I'm in. What do we do next?"

Chapter Seven

Zayn knew what the little man had been thinking when he'd left the officers' club, but he had no intention of going along with the plan to marry him off without making one final attempt to get reassigned. He made his way to the bridge and walked on without permission, hoping he'd find a sympathetic ear in the space station's captain. If he could get a commanding officer in his corner, he'd stand a better chance of getting off the station.

Heads swiveled toward him when he walked in, and he took in uniformed warriors posted below hanging screens and at standing metal consoles that looked out onto a wide, glass wall with a view of the stars. He found the spartan bridge comforting, after the luxury of the fantasy suite and the pristine common spaces. This felt like the Drexian ships he knew. Sounded like it, too—the beeps, the static from transmissions, the tapping of fingers on consoles. Zayn closed his eyes for a moment to drink it all in, opening them when he heard loud footsteps pounding toward him.

"Zayn of House Toreth." It was a statement, not a question from the warrior who approached him.

Zayn gave him a chest salute when he saw the stripes indicating his status as ship's captain. "Yes, sir. I believe you have me at a disadvantage."

The captain returned his salute. "Captain Varden. I know of your escape."

Zayn nodded, knowing the captain would also have been briefed on his failed mission and his dead platoon.

"It's good to see you back among us." The captain's eyes paused for a moment on Zayn's scarred arms.

"Thank you, sir," Zayn said. "I came to request a favor."

The captain dragged a hand through his hair, the flash of silver strands glinting. "You know I have no influence over the tribute bride program. If they've matched you with a wild one like they did with—"

"It isn't about the brides," Zayn said, not meaning to cut the man off, but feeling desperate to plead his case. "It's about my mission. I need to get back out there."

"You want to go back after what they did to you?"

Zayn bit the inside of his cheek and tasted blood. "I need to avenge my fallen comrades." He didn't say that he suspected he was being kept on the station and away from missions on purpose. He knew it would sound crazy. Unless the captain was in on it.

Varden nodded. "I can understand that, but I don't have the authority to assign you."

Panic fluttered in Zayn's chest. "I thought you could put in a good word for me. Maybe recommend me for a mission. Convince High Commander Kax to let me join his." He clutched the man's arm. "I can't stay here and pretend everything's all right. Not after what I saw."

The captain placed a hand over his. "Kax of House Baraat is no longer a High Commander, but he has just left on his mission near Kronock territory."

Zayn glanced at the view of space as though he might see Kax's ship flying by. "When? Maybe I could catch up to him?"

The captain walked him toward the door. "Why don't I speak to someone for you? I doubt you could catch Kax, but I will convey your wishes to be reassigned."

Zayn studied the man. He felt like he was being humored, but he didn't sense deception in the captain. If there was a plan to keep him on the station for a reason that didn't involve tribute brides, he didn't think this Drexian was part of it. "Do you give me your word?"

The captain's expression flickered for a moment, before he gave a curt nod. "I give you my word. Now, the best thing for you to do is rest so you'll be ready when you're called up."

The door slid open, and Zayn found himself back in the bright corridor. He made his way back down to the fantasy-suite level, barely noticing the human females passing him this time. He swiped his hand over the door panel and went inside, bracing himself to find the Earthling with whom he'd been matched.

The open-air room was empty and quiet; the only sounds that of the birds flapping by the balcony and animals walking through the tall grasses. He sat on the edge of the bed, trying to block out the images that kept flashing through his mind. Images of his fellow warriors falling. The sounds of their screams as they were killed.

Maybe the High Command was right to keep him away from battle. The pain in his body was nothing compared to the pain he experienced every time he closed his eyes. His body would heal. He didn't know if this grief and guilt would ever leave him. A mirthless laugh escaped his lips. How could they think a tribute bride could make everything better?

Didn't they see he didn't deserve her? Rewarding him with a pretty female after he'd failed his fellow warriors felt like having silver nitrate rubbed into his wounds. Kax pressed the heels of his hands to his eyes until his head ached. He stood, crossed to the standing dresser, and found a pair of drawstring pants in a drawer. He walked into the bathroom, peeling off his clothes as he went, and tossing the clean pants on the marble counter.

Maybe hot water would help, he thought as he eyed the open-air shower next to the freestanding tub. He swiped a hand across a control panel and waited for the water to heat before stepping under it, and then he leaned his arms against the one glass wall as the water pounded down his head and back. The heat stung his skin, but he welcomed the pain. It kept his mind off the real agony playing out in his head.

As the water spilled over his back, he felt the nodes on his spine warm. He'd learned that humans didn't have bumps along their spine that signaled arousal, or could trigger arousal if stimulated. As the beating water caressed his nodes, he felt bad that humans lacked this pleasure center, and he bowed his back so the water hit him more directly. He groaned as his cock began to engorge in response. He took himself in one fist, dragging his hand up and down his shaft as the water beat on him. Desire coiled in his spine, and an image of his tribute bride flashed through his mind. He pumped harder as he thought of her fiery hair and the curves barely concealed by her thin dress. He imagined himself tearing the dress off her to reveal more of her creamy skin, and he felt his release building. As he pictured himself burying his cock between her legs, he exploded, arching his head back as he cried out.

When he'd stopped convulsing, he stood under the torrent for a few more moments before turning it off and wrapping a fluffy towel around his waist. He hadn't even known how desirable he found the human female until he'd imagined her beneath him. His cock twitched again, but he pushed the thoughts away. The knots in his shoulders had relaxed, and he felt the built-up exhaustion begin to overtake him. He returned to the empty bedroom and crawled into bed, dropping the towel on the floor and pulling the ivory sheets up over his naked body. He hadn't had anything this soft touch his skin in longer than he could remember. He burrowed deeper, letting out a long breath and allowing his eyes to flutter closed as he drifted into sleep, hoping he would dream of the human.

Almost immediately, he was back in the battle with the Kronock. He could smell the singed flesh and taste the metallic sharpness of blood in his mouth. Bodies lay around him, some Kronock and some Drexian. He stumbled over them as he fought one of his scaled enemies, ducking as the creature swiped at him with a clawed hand. Both fighters had lost their blasters and had to rely on hand-to-hand combat. Zayn landed a hard kick to the Kronock's armored abdomen, but it had little effect. Out of the corner of his eye, he could see one of his fellow officers firing a blaster at more incoming Kronock before taking a long blade through the belly.

Zayn felt his breath leave him as the Drexian fell. He tried to reach him, but his legs wouldn't move. He could feel the Kronock grab him, but he pulled away. He had to get the fallen warrior. Had to get him out of the way. Maybe the blade had gotten him in the side, and he could be saved. If only Zayn's legs would move. Why wouldn't his legs move? He thrashed as he fought off the Kronock pursuing him, finally pinning the creature beneath him and being surprised by the high-pitched screams.

Chapter Eight

Katie tried to pull the shopping bags out of Reina's hands. "I'm perfectly capable of carrying my own bags."

Reina tugged back, keeping her long fingers wrapped vise-like around the ribbon handles. "It's my job to make the process easier for you. I'm your liaison. Serge may handle most of the planning, but I make sure your needs are taken care of."

Katie raised her hands in mock surrender. "Then I give."

"I hope your mate likes the outfits you selected," Reina said, peering into the bags as she led the way down the wooden walkway.

Katie nodded, casting a glance at the alfresco bar down a shorter walkway. A stone fire pit sat to one side, with the square wooden bar under a high-peaked tent. The fire crackled, and she could smell the wood burning, although she suspected the flames weren't real and the scent was manufactured. Glancing over the green field past the bar, she saw the sun dipping low behind the far trees. The fading light was warm, and cast long shadows across the grass and spread a golden glow on everything it touched. A pair of gazelles ran by, and a long-beaked bird glided through the air above.

"Tell me again how much of this is real," she said to Reina.

"The Drexian holographic technology is very advanced. Everything you see, you can touch and experience." Reina waved a hand at the fire pit. "For instance, the fire could burn you although they are not actual flames."

"So, no *Star Trek* safety protocols to prevent me from dying out here?"

Reina's eyes grew large. "We would never let you die."

"I'm kidding." Katie patted the alien's arm, her eyes drifting to the shopping bags. She didn't want to think about the items inside. The ones she'd selected for the sole purpose of seducing her alien fiancé. "You know what? We should have a drink before I head back to the suite."

"We should?" Reina looked around her. "You and me?"

Katie shrugged. "Why not? Don't you hang out with your other clients?"

"Brides," Reina corrected her. "And not usually. They're either busy with their Drexian warriors, or they choose to socialize with the other tribute brides. It is a rare occurrence for me to socialize alone with a tribute."

Katie pulled her by the sleeve as she headed down the walkway. "Well, then, those brides don't know what they're missing. I think you and I both need a drink."

"I suppose one drink would be fine."

Katie hopped up on a bar stool and patted the seat next to her, then gave the bartender her most charming smile. "What do you recommend for two girls who want to loosen up a bit?"

TANA STONE

"I don't know if I'd say loosen up…" Reina stammered, as she gathered the shopping bags around her feet and sat down next to Katie.

The tall, thin man, with skin the same shade as Reina's, placed two paper napkins on the bar. "We have Palaxian Punch, which is made with Palaxian Pl—"

"Sounds perfect," Katie said, giving him another smile that she usually saved for marks, as she palmed her cocktail napkin. "Two of those."

Reina glanced behind her as a couple approached and sat down around the fire pit, her hands fluttering to her throat. The man was clearly Drexian, with wide shoulders and bronze skin, and the woman was human, and they seemed completely besotted.

Katie looked away and focused on the light-orange drinks being set in front of them. "So you can't tell me every couple that's matched gets along."

Reina took a hesitant sip of her drink. "Not all, of course, but many are quite compatible. It was lucky for the Drexians that human biology is so similar to theirs. Otherwise they'd be extinct."

"So all Drexian babies born now are half Drexian-half human?"

Reina tilted her head. "I suppose so. I've heard there are some Drexian females back on the home world, but very few, and they are advanced in age."

"Do any couples ever go back to the Drexian home world?"

Reina took a longer sip. "The home world was all but destroyed generations ago. Only some elders and purists remain."

"Purists?" Katie asked, taking a drink of the Palaxian Punch and thinking it tasted like liquid cotton candy.

Reina dropped her voice. "Drexians who don't believe in mixing with humans."

"Are there a lot of those?" Katie asked, slightly distracted that her fingers were beginning to tingle.

Reina shook her head. "No. Even most Drexians who find humans to be inferior have acknowledged they're necessary to continue the species."

"Glad we could help out," Katie said, sure that Reina didn't get her sarcasm. She looked over at the couple nuzzling by the fire. "So back to the couples that don't get along."

"Why? Do you think you won't get along with your mate? If so, I'm not sure you selected the right type of clothing."

Katie shrugged and tried to sound nonchalant. "Just curious, that's all. What if a human can't stand the guy she's matched with, or if the guy thinks his human is annoying?"

Reina leaned one arm on the bar. "There have been occasions when brides have been given new matches. Very rarely, a bride refuses the concept entirely."

"A Drexian has never rejected a match?" Katie asked. Her experience with men made that very difficult for her to believe. "They've always been fine with the human they're matched with?"

"As far as I know. Duty and honor are very important to Drexians. I think it would be considered dishonorable to reject a match."

Interesting, thought Katie. Aliens who made it a habit to kidnap humans but had a strong sense of honor. She'd have to be sure to touch on that in her exposé. "And the humans who refuse to go along with any of it?"

Reina bit the edge of her lip. "They're housed in a separate section of the station."

Katie nudged the alien. "I'll bet it isn't as nice as this, is it?"

Reina gave a furtive shake of her head. "I do not think so."

Katie took another small sip, being sure to drink less than her companion. One rule for drawing information out of someone. Never be drunker than they were.

"Is it on the top level?" Katie asked.

Reina gave a tinkling laugh. "The top level? That's where the bridge and officers' lounge is. No, the section with the unmated tribute brides is one level above the staff quarters at the bottom."

Katie made a note on the cocktail napkin in her lap with the pen she'd swiped earlier from one of the shops. "So like a cruise ship, with the fancy cabins at the top and the cheapest ones at the bottom?"

Reina wrinkled her nose. "A cruise ship?"

"Don't you call this place the Boat?"

Another laugh from Reina. "You are right. *The Love Boat* was a program about a cruise ship."

"True, but what does *The Love Boat* have to do with anything?" Katie asked, wiggling her toes and feeling them tingle.

"The designers of this space station used a lot of Earth media to inspire them."

"And out of all Earth movies and TV, they settled on *The Love Boat*?" Katie threw back her head and laughed. "That explains a lot. When do we have shuffleboard on the Lido deck?"

Reina joined her in laughing, but looked confused. "I do not know this Lido deck."

"Don't sweat it." Katie made a final covert note on her napkin, stood, and scooped up the bags before her liaison could protest. "I'd better get back to my suite. Those drinks pack a punch."

Reina tried to stand, but ended up sliding and catching herself on the edge of the bar with her spindly legs splayed out in front of her. "Wait for me."

Katie hoisted her up by the arm and plopped her back on her barstool. She caught the bartender's eye. "Make sure she doesn't leave until she can walk, will you?"

Reina lay her head down on the bar. "Maybe you're right. I'm feeling awfully sleepy."

Katie watched, as the blue-haired woman began snoring. She patted her gently on the back and glanced at the cocktail napkin folded in one hand with her notes. "Sweet dreams. Thanks for the info."

She walked as quickly as she could, considering how tipsy she felt, waving her hand over the panel by her door and going inside. The sun had set and the room was dark, the only light coming from the moon outside and a few lanterns on the balcony. Katie dropped the bags on the floor when she didn't see any sign of Zayn, and kicked off her shoes. She pulled off her dress and bra, stepped out of her panties, and walked to the far side of the bed—the side she always slept on—and tucked her cocktail-napkin notes into a drawer in the nightstand.

Her mind was reeling with everything she'd learned, but she was also worn out. Between being drugged and transported across the solar system, and walking around the massive space station, her body ached. She pushed aside the sheer netting over the bed and slipped under the covers, not caring that she was naked since she was alone in the room. She'd always slept naked, anyway.

Rolling over, she bumped something warm and big, and she froze. Her heart racing, she reached out and touched the side of a massive person. Further exploration by her fingers told that this person was a man and was also naked. She assumed it was Zayn, and she felt her irritation rise. Who did he think he was, getting in bed naked? She tried to ignore the fact the she herself was naked, reasoning that it was only because she thought he wasn't coming back. Maybe he believed the same thing, she thought.

He started mumbling in his sleep, his voice agitated, and she jerked her hand away.

Katie sat up as he began crying out, thrashing in the bed. From the faint light spilling in from the balcony, she could see his face contorted in obvious pain. Was there an emergency call button somewhere? She doubted it.

"I'm coming for you," he mumbled. "Hold on."

More thrashing, followed by a keening sound that gave her goose bumps. She didn't know what he was dreaming about, but he was clearly distressed. Did this have anything to do with the scars on his arm? She reached out and put a hand on his chest. "It's okay. You're dreaming."

"I won't let you kill him," Zayn cried. Without opening his eyes, he grasped her wrist and flipped her on her back. His muscular body was pressed flush against hers, and she could feel his cock as it hardened between her thighs. He held her down, his weight pressing her wrists into the mattress and causing her to scream out in pain.

"Get off me!" She fought to pull free, but his grip was too tight.

His face was only inches from hers when he opened his eyes and blinked a few times. It seemed to take him a minute to determine he wasn't wherever he'd thought he was, then all the fight left him and he went limp on her, burying his head in her neck and scooping his arms under her to pull her closer as he trembled violently.

Even though he was no longer flailing, his body shook as he held her against him, and Katie could still feel his firm cock between her legs. She could also feel her body's traitorous response to rubbing up on him—her nipples were hard against his chest, and she was wet between her thighs.

"Zayn," she whispered. "If you're okay, would you mind letting me go?"

His arms stiffened, and he pulled away from her, looking down at her naked body and his own and rolling off her and out of bed.

Katie pulled the sheet up to cover herself, watching as he whipped a towel off the floor and wrapped it around his waist. But not before she got a glimpse of what had been pressing against her leg —thick and long enough to make her mouth go dry.

"I'm sorry," Zayn stammered. "I didn't mean to…I didn't know…I never would have…"

As he disappeared into the bathroom, Katie wasn't sure if she was more curious about what he'd been dreaming about, or what was beneath his towel.

Chapter Nine

Zayn stumbled into the bathroom and leaned against the marble sink, his breathing jagged. He looked at himself in the mirror and flinched. His hair was wild, his body glistened with sweat, and his cock stood out ramrod straight from his body. Balling his fists, he fought the desire coursing through him.

What had happened out there? How had she ended up in bed with him? The better question was, how she'd ended up naked and pinned underneath him.

Zayn dragged a hand over his face and turned from the mirror. He couldn't bear to look at himself. Had he really been so out of it that he'd nearly taken her without even being aware of it? He squeezed his eyes shut as he thought of her terrified expression when he'd finally realized where he was, when he'd looked down and seen her naked breasts, with her hard, pink nipples, and felt her slick thighs enveloping his cock.

He groaned and crossed to the shower, turning on the water to cold and plunging himself under the bracing flow. His breath caught in his throat as the icy water hit him, but after a few gasps he welcomed the relief as his body cooled. His cock, however, would not obey the rest of his body, and Zayn knew it was because of her. He couldn't get the image of her out of his mind—her full breasts, her narrow waist, the swell of her hips. He also couldn't dismiss the way her body had reacted to his, even as he tried to suppress the feeling of her wet heat.

"Stop it," he said to himself. He couldn't let himself get distracted by a female, no matter how alluring she was. He needed to focus on uncovering the truth behind why he was here and not back out in the field.

You know why, he thought, as he pressed both hands against the glass wall of the shower. Images of the human female left his mind to be replaced by flashes of his fellow warriors falling around him. Bile rose in his throat as he replayed the scene in his mind. No matter how many times he tried to recreate the battle in his head, his friends always ended up dead. No matter how often he reviewed the scenario, it was always his fault.

He turned off the water and stepped out, toweling off and getting into the drawstring pants he'd left on the counter earlier. The soft fabric was a welcome change from his usual stiff military pants, even if they left little to the imagination.

Returning to the suite, he chanced a glance at the bed. Empty. He felt his stomach clench. He hoped she wasn't running around the station wrapped up in a sheet screaming about the maniac who'd attacked her. Not that he didn't deserve it, he thought.

Zayn walked out onto the balcony where the holographic moon shone high in the night sky, illuminating a flat-topped tree. Even if it wasn't real, the grass rustling in the soft breeze and the caw of a distant bird made his shoulders relax. He knew the holographic environments were modeled after places on Earth, and if that was true, the planet his people protected must be worth defending if it was filled with such a peaceful place. He leaned his forearms on the wooden railing and rubbed a hand absently over his scars.

"So those are the famous nodes?"

Her voice from behind startled him, and he spun around to find her nestled in one of the wood-and-canvas lounge chairs, wrapped in the blanket that had been draped across the foot of the bed. Her mane of curls cascaded down her shoulders, the moonlight reflecting off it. He stared at her for a moment, expecting her to begin shouting at him or at the very least to ask him to leave. "What?"

She pointed at his bare back and he twisted his neck to look at himself. "Oh, my nodes." He brushed one hand over the bumps that ran all the way down his spinal cord.

"Interesting. Is it ever uncomfortable to have bumps on your back?"

Zayn was glad the lighting was dim and she couldn't see his face warm. "Only when they harden and heat, but that's only uncomfortable if I can't…"

"Oh," she said, a small smile playing around the corners of her mouth. "So, not so different from humans, after all."

As her eyes went to his back again, he concentrated on *not* getting aroused by breathing in the cool night air and blowing it out through his mouth. "I owe you an apology," he said, the words tumbling out in a rush.

She motioned to the canvas lounge chair next to hers. "For pretending to be sleeping so you could jump me?"

"No." He sat down, angling so he faced her. "I was sleeping. I didn't know—"

"Relax." She held up her palms. "I'm teasing you. Trying to make light of the situation so it isn't so awkward that we almost, well, that you almost sleep-fucked me."

Zayn cleared his throat and looked down. He didn't know human females talked like that. "Is that something that happens on your planet?"

"No." She laughed. "I mean, maybe to some. Not to me, though."

"Are you a typical Earth female?" he asked. Since he'd never applied for a tribute bride, he didn't know much about human females. Even without knowing much, she wasn't what he'd expected. "I have never seen hair the color of yours. Or skin so pale."

She laughed. "Yeah, I've never had a tan in my entire life. Most humans aren't as pasty white as I am, but we come in lots of different shades."

"And hair colors?"

"That, too," she said. "Everything from black to blonde to gray. Even more with dyes. I'm what we call a strawberry blonde."

"Strawberry blonde," he repeated, staring at her curls. "It looks like fire."

"Thanks, I think. I got called Little Orphan Annie a lot." She pulled at one of her curls and it sprang back as she released it. "I'm more strawberry than blonde, which does not make it easy to blend in."

"Is it typical for humans? The others I've seen don't have it."

She shrugged. "I don't know if there's such a thing as a typical woman. We're all pretty different. I guess as far as American women go, I'm not the norm."

"No?" Zayn leaned forward. "Are you abnormal?"

Another laugh, and she pulled the blanket tighter around her shoulders. "Not physically. But let's just say I had an unusual childhood. There was no white, picket fence or dog named Spot in the world I came from."

He wasn't sure what any of that meant, but before he could ask, she shook her head like she was trying to dislodge something.

"What about you?" she asked. "Care to tell me why you have such wild nightmares?"

It was impossible to deny, since she'd seen him as he'd been reliving the horror in his sleep. Despite replaying the battle again and again, it was hard to find words to explain it and explain why it haunted him. But he knew she deserved some explanation, and her soft voice, which held no trace of blame or anger, made him want tell her the truth.

He cleared his throat, and it felt like sandpaper. "I led a high-level military unit. We'd been together for years."

"Like the Navy SEALs or Delta Force?"

"We didn't have a special name, but our job was to take out high-priority targets and gather information from places that were difficult to get into. The Kronock are notoriously paranoid and xenophobic, so gathering useful information was a challenge."

"Those are the aliens who tried to invade Earth, right?"

Zayn nodded. "Their main goal seems to be to invade a planet, strip it of its resources, enslave or assimilate its people, and move on. We've battled them all over the galaxy."

Katie shuddered. "So you were trying to find out what they were up to?"

"We suspected they'd been making advancements in their technology, but we didn't know how, or what they were. They didn't demonstrate any changes in the ships that engaged ours, but we'd intercepted chatter about a lab. It took us months to determine where it was and gather enough intelligence to get close." He took a shaky breath. "Since it was such a crucial mission, we all went in."

Zayn closed his eyes as he remembered the shouts of surprise and the smell the burning flesh as his team was ambushed. "They knew we were coming. It was a trap we never anticipated. Everyone on my team was killed except for me. Me, they kept to torture."

He felt her hand close around his. "I'm really sorry."

He didn't meet her eyes. "I was the leader. I should have known better. I should have protected my team." He stood abruptly and let her hand fall from his. "It's my fault they're dead."

"I think you're being too tough on yourself."

"I was their leader, and I didn't protect them. My punishment is having to hear their screams in my head every time I close my eyes, but still, it isn't enough."

Katie stood and joined him at the railing, touching one of the faded slashes on his arm. "You were tortured. Don't you think that was punishment?"

"I took their torture gladly, hoping it would one day kill me, and I could join my team."

She gave a low whistle. "That's pretty hardcore. You never talked?"

"They never asked me," he said. "I always thought they would, but they never did. They seemed to torture me for the sport of it."

"Harsh," she said under her breath.

He twitched one shoulder up. "Their torture is nothing compared to reliving my friends' deaths. And now the High Command won't let me return to the field where I belong. They're punishing me, too." He swept an arm wide. "This is part of my punishment."

"So that's what you were talking about earlier. You never wanted any of this. This whole tribute bride thing was as much of a shock for you as it was for me."

"Perhaps a bit less for me since I knew tribute brides existed. I just never desired one for myself."

"Really?" She backed away from the railing. "You're trying to tell me you don't desire me?"

He heard the mocking in her voice. It would be foolish to deny that he was attracted to her when he'd been lying on top of her with a rock-hard erection. "It's not that I don't desire you, but you're too beautiful for someone like me."

"Someone like you?"

"I'm damaged." He slammed a hand on the wood rail before turning to face her. "A disgraced warrior."

The blanket slipped down, exposing one alabaster shoulder, and she smiled at him. "You don't look so damaged to me, and I've always been a sucker for an underdog."

As he watched the soft light silhouette her body, Zayn couldn't speak.

Chapter Ten

Katie padded back into the bedroom, glancing over her shoulder at the big alien on the balcony. The moonlight bounced off his muscular body, and the outline of his broad shoulders and narrow hips made her pulse flutter. She squinted in the dark, her heart clenching as she turned away.

She'd been honest when she'd said she always liked an underdog. It was why running cons had been so hard for her. She had a tough time working marks unless she thought they deserved it. Nothing her father had said had made it any easier, either, which was why he'd rarely used her in his long cons. She didn't have any issue conning a bad guy, or someone who had it coming. Cheating the slumlord who'd been screwing over his residents, or tricking the man who treated his wife badly? It hadn't bothered her one bit when her father had lightened the pockets of those people, but this guy wasn't bad. She could feel it. He was just hurt and a little lost. Like her.

Get a grip, Katie told herself. Even if he was the greatest guy in the universe she still needed to use him to get what she needed. And what she needed was to get off the space station and get back to

Earth. The alternative was living with aliens for the rest of her life. As cool as the Boat was, it was almost too perfect for someone like her who'd grown up on the gritty side of the street. She hadn't done anything to deserve a life of luxury with a gorgeous guy, and so far everyone up on the station seemed too perfect. She didn't fit in.

Katie ignored the bed, as well as the knot in her stomach, walking to the sitting area to the side of the bedroom and lowering herself into one of the ebony rattan chairs positioned on top of the Persian rug. In the moonlight, the colors of the rug were muted, but she could still make out the geometric patterns and feel the tight weave on her bare feet. Another section of the balcony extended to the side, with cream-colored curtains tied back to reveal more open savannah. A cluster of gardenia trees grew up next to the railing, the perfume of their white blooms drifting inside.

She had to give it to these Drexians. Their holographic recreation was amazing. Between the distant sounds of animals and the smell of impending rain she could almost taste, it was hard to believe she wasn't back on Earth. Would anyone believe her when she did blow the lid off this project? It was a challenge to wrap her head around it even as she was experiencing it, much less believe the far-fetched idea without hard evidence.

"I'll just have to get evidence," she murmured to herself, missing her camera for the hundredth time that day.

She twisted her neck to see Zayn still standing at the other railing, his massive form casting a long shadow across the polished wood of the floor. Why did she feel so guilty already? She hadn't done anything. Not yet at least.

But you will, the little voice in her head told her. *You'll have to use him to get the information you need. If you're going to be a believable tribute bride, you'll have to convince him and everyone else.*

She let her head fall back against the chair's cushion and closed her eyes, even though she knew sleep wouldn't come. Not when she felt like this. She let out a breath and tried to will the knot in her gut to unclench. Even though she hated always looking at people as marks, she couldn't help it. It had been imprinted on her so young, she wondered if she was even capable of caring for someone without having an angle. Which was probably why all her boyfriends had been losers or jerks. She couldn't let herself get close to someone truly good because she knew she'd end up hurting them. Of course her latest, Mark, had beaten her to it, but she would have used him and left him if he hadn't done the same to her first.

She rubbed a hand over her forehead, feeling the creases that formed when she worried. At this rate she was going to be wrinkled mess before she was thirty.

The crackling sound made her eyes fly open as the sky flickered and the savannah disappeared for a moment, revealing the domed ceiling covered in white tiles. Katie jerked up, expecting the furniture under her to vanish, but it remained, although the soothing thrum of rain in the distance disappeared. The environment reappeared almost as quickly as it had dissolved.

She looked around muttering, "What the hell was that?"

Zayn crossed the room, one hand pressed to his temple. "Are you okay?"

"I'm fine." She watched him knead his temple. "Are you?"

He dropped his hand from his head. "I'm sure it was a brief malfunction. Probably a residual effect from the Kronock attack."

"The what?"

"Our sworn enemy mounted a failed attack on this station a little while ago. Some systems were damaged, so this is probably a result of that."

"Sworn enemy?" Katie suppressed the urge to giggle, even though she knew he wasn't joking.

"Yes." Zayn's face was solemn. "We've kept the Kronock at bay for decades, but if they succeeded it would be the end of your planet."

The laughter died in her throat. "Oh, right." It was hard to imagine that violent aliens were hell-bent on destroying Earth, and no one on the surface had any idea. Not yet at least. "Should I be worried?"

"The Boat is probably safe for now."

"That's a ringing endorsement," she said under her breath, then held a hand over her mouth as she yawned.

"You can take the bed. You need to sleep."

"Thanks, but I can't sleep right now."

"You're worried I'll…" he began, then paused and exhaled loudly. "I promise I won't touch you again."

"Ever?" She cocked an eyebrow. "That's a pretty big promise, considering we're supposed to be mated."

"I don't want to hurt you." His voice was hoarse. "I need to protect you, even from myself."

"I'm not afraid of you. I know you won't hurt me." She craned her head to look up, tipping her neck back to take in all of him. As she said the words, she realized she believed them completely. "It's not you. It's that my mind won't let me sleep."

"Do not worry about the Kronock. The Drexians will fight to the death to protect the station."

The intensity of his words made her instinctively feel better. "It isn't that."

"Do you get nightmares?" He took the overstuffed rattan love seat across from her, his massive arms extending across the entire length as he stretched them out behind him.

"Not exactly, but sometimes memories haunt me." She shifted in her chair, surprised she'd admitted so much to a virtual stranger.

He studied her face and nodded. "People you've lost?"

She shrugged. More like people she'd hurt.

"Tell me about your life on Earth, Katie." He said her name in two distinct syllables, Kay-tee, making it sound exotic rather than commonplace.

"Not much exciting to tell," she said, "especially compared to all this."

He leaned forward and rested his elbows on his knees. "This is not normal for Drexians, either. Most of us spend our lives on battle-ships or military outposts."

"You're all soldiers?" Her eyes dropped to his scarred arms and away again before he could notice her staring.

He dipped his head in a curt nod. "We are a warrior race known throughout the galaxy for protecting other species from violence. It's why we battle the Kronock and protect Earth."

"I thought you protected Earth so you could get women."

"All the planets we save contribute to our greater purpose," Zayn said. "Our scientists, artisans, and workers all come from races we've rescued."

He sounded like he was spouting lines from a brochure, Katie thought. "And all your women come from Earth." She tilted her head at him. "So when you guys ride in on the cavalry to save other planets, it's not completely altruistic."

It was his turn to angle his head at her. "Cavalry?"

She waved a hand. "I guess it's an Earth thing."

"You were going to tell me about Earth." He reclined on the cream-colored couch cushions again.

"Was I?" She tucked her feet under her. "Well, it's not like this, but I guess since you guys modeled the holographs after Earth, it is like this. At least parts of it. I've never been to Africa, but I've heard it's beautiful."

"What was it like where you lived?"

"LA?" She laughed. "Big, loud, crowded, busy. Important people always going somewhere in a rush."

"Were you happy there?"

His question caught her off guard. She couldn't claim she'd been happy sneaking around, trying to catch celebrities in embarrassing moments. And Mark was cute enough, but he'd never made her happy. Had she ever been happy? Really, truly happy? That was easy. "No, but I was too busy trying to pay the rent and keep gas in my car to think about it."

"Happiness is a luxury I've never had, either."

She looked hard at the shirtless man sitting across from her, with his massive bare arms and rippled stomach. He seemed a lot more insightful than she would have expected, although she didn't have much experience with alien warriors to base her opinion off of. She knew she shouldn't assume he was empty-headed because he was so good-looking, but living around so many beautiful, brainless people in LA had not helped. "You aren't what I'd expect."

"I do not understand. I thought you didn't know about Drexians until today."

Thunder rumbled in the distance, but she suspected the fake rain would never reach them.

"I used to photograph famous people on Earth," she said, trying to explain. "People who were beautiful, with great bodies, who were paid to look great on screen. Some were okay, but a lot of them were full of themselves and a pain in the ass. I guess I got used to seeing people like you and expecting them to be divas."

"Like me?" He furrowed his brow.

"You know." Her eyes dropped to his chest and she felt her face warm. "Hard-bodied and beautiful."

"I am hardly beautiful." He frowned. "You are not one of the beautiful people on Earth?"

A burst of laughter escaped her throat, louder than she would have liked, and she clamped a hand over her mouth. "Not movie star beautiful."

Zayn's face contorted and he raised his hands to his temples. The holographic suite flickered again, and they were sitting under the white dome once more. The lights went off, thrusting them into darkness before the entire system came on again and the idyllic setting returned.

"What was that?" she asked.

"The malfunctions are increasing," he said, giving his head an almost imperceptible shake.

"I don't mean that," Katie said. "I mean your head. You looked like you were in pain right before it happened. Could you sense it?"

A confused expression crossed his face. "I don't think so. How could that be possible?"

She shrugged, but didn't take her eyes off him. Something else was going on. She was adept enough at reading people to know that

Zayn genuinely had no idea why he'd been able to sense the station's glitch before it happened, but she also didn't believe in coincidences.

Now, she not only needed to get enough evidence for her story, she also needed to figure out what was really going on with Zayn.

Chapter Eleven

"Rise and shine, lovebirds!"

Zayn looked up from where he'd curled up on the love seat, his long legs bunched up and his chest hanging halfway off the cushions. He braced himself with one hand on the floor before he rolled off entirely.

The purple-haired Gatazoid from the day before led a small procession into the suite, waving at the one Vexling guiding the hovering breakfast cart and the other holding a clear clipboard. He directed the Vexling to leave the breakfast before tapping one hot-pink platform boot on the gleaming wooden floors.

Zayn breathed in the savory scents coming from the hover cart, his growling stomach a reminder that he'd drunk more than he'd eaten the day before. Blinking hard, he scanned the room until he saw a mess of red curls tangled with the bed sheets, his heart beating faster at the thought of her under the soft bedding.

"What…?" The remaining Vexling looked from the towel in a pile beside the bed to him on the love seat to the red hair peeking above the sheets.

The Gatazoid—Serge, that was the little alien's name—elbowed her. "Not now, Reina. We need to focus."

Katie lifted her head and moaned, flopping back down and pulling the sheets back up over her face. "Is there coffee?"

"Coffee?" Reina asked, glancing at the silver domes covering the hover cart. "We have moi-moi juice, which is delicious and filled with nutrients. Do you require a morning stimulant?"

The lump under the sheets moaned again. "Whatever you need to call it, I need it."

Zayn stood and stretched his arms up over his head, his hands nearly brushing the inside of the tented ceiling. He crossed to the cart filled with food and began lifting the shiny domes off plates. One thing he could say about the Boat, the food was excellent. Picking up a slice of fried padwump, he bit into it and closed his eyes to savor the salty flavor.

Opening his eyes, he found Reina and Serge gaping at him. He swallowed and realized his drawstring pants had slipped down below his hips; the only thing holding them up was his substantial erection. He tugged his pants higher and spun around.

"Now then," Serge said, clapping his hands. "I believe I mentioned the dress appointment yesterday. There's no time to waste, Katie."

Zayn knew seeing the human getting out of bed would do nothing to reduce his arousal, so he plucked a glass of juice from the cart and walked out to the balcony. A group of black-and-white-striped animals grazed near the railing, and he focused on them so he wouldn't think about the half-naked woman in his bed. The sounds of the birds cawing and hooves thudding on the ground distracted him from the noises of Serge rousing Katie inside the room.

"There we go. A nice little nibble and then off to the shower with you."

He refused to turn. He heard the sounds of domes being lifted off plates and could imagine what she looked like standing with the sheet draped around her well enough. If picturing her wrapped in a sheet made his heart race, he did not want to know what would happen if he actually saw her.

The noise of the shower being activated was followed by a yelp, and Zayn couldn't help laughing. Nothing like cold water to wake you up.

Now that she was out of the bedroom, he turned and walked back to the food. Reina was gone, he assumed helping Katie get ready since she was female, but Serge stood waiting outside the bathroom door.

Zayn pointed to the plates of food. "Hungry? There's more than enough."

The little man shook his head. "Thank you, but no. I had the chef prepare a little bit of everything since we didn't know what she liked to eat."

Zayn poked at a shiny ring on a square plate.

"From what I understand," Serge said, "that is called a doughnut. Very popular breakfast food on Earth. Apparently, your bride is a fan."

Zayn picked it up by two fingers and took a bite. The ring was soft, sticky, and so sweet he flinched as he swallowed.

Serge gave him a knowing look. "Humans love sugar."

Zayn put the rest of the sugary ring back on the plate and licked his fingers.

Serge thrust a napkin at him. "Here, sweetie. You may have nailed the warrior vibe, but let's not scare the female." He shifted from one platform boot to the other as he watched Zayn wipe his mouth. "Is everything okay with you and the tribute?"

"Fine." No way would be admit what had happened last night, although he wouldn't blame her if Katie told someone.

"If there's a problem, I'd rather know now, than after I've spent days planning a wedding," Serge said. "You have no idea how excruciating it is to have to see a wedding design go to waste."

Zayn wasn't sure what the alien meant, but he noticed the roots of his hair turning pink as he bounced up and down.

"Listen," Serge said, leaning close to him. "I know you weren't on the list to get a tribute, so all this must come as a surprise, but from what I hear, no Drexian needs this more than you do."

Zayn felt his stomach tighten. What had the Gatazoid heard about him? Did he know he'd been the only one of his team to survive? Did he know he'd left a Drexian back in a Kronock prison?

"If you're one of those purists who doesn't believe in mating with humans, or if you find their lack of a third breast off-putting, tell me now." Serge tapped his foot. "I can work a lot of magic, but giving your tribute an extra breast is beyond even my abilities."

"No," he said. "Katie is acceptable."

Serge cocked an eyebrow. "Well, aren't you the sweet-talker?" He gave Zayn the once-over. "I suppose you have other qualities."

So the Gatazoid could see it too? He didn't belong here, and he certainly didn't deserve a tribute as pretty as Katie. He wasn't sure at this point if he hoped he would be discovered as a fraud or if he was terrified of it.

"We're ready," Reina called out, as she and Katie emerged from the bathroom bringing a cloud of steam and a flowery scent with them.

Zayn was glad he'd put down the sticky ring, or he surely would have dropped it.

Katie wore a silky, green top, and a black skirt that hugged her curves. Her feet were in high, strappy shoes that showed off her long legs and lightly tapped the floor when she walked. Her hair had been pulled half up so that he noticed the soft green shade of her eyes.

His mouth was parched as he tried to speak and failed.

She walked toward him, twisting her hips with each step—something she had not done the night before. Her eyes locked with his, and she smiled at him. "I'll be back later. Don't miss me too much, hot stuff."

He reflexively stepped back, startled by the transformation. This was not the introspective woman he'd talked to the night before.

Katie leaned in, placing her palms on his chest. Her touch jolted him, the warmth and softness of her hands electric against his bare skin.

Her expression faltered, and she glanced at her hands, and then looked back up at him. With a determined look in her eye, she grabbed the back of his neck and pulled him down to her. Their lips brushed, and he felt this jolt like a shockwave. His body hummed as he responded, crushing his mouth to hers and feeling her yield to him as his tongue parted her lips. Her breathless moan made him wrap his arms around her, sweeping her off the floor and holding her tight to him. The sweet taste of her caused the blood to pound in his ears, and only the feel of her nails digging into his chest brought him back to reality.

He dropped her, stepping back and gasping for air. She staggered away from him, the seductive smile gone from her face.

"My, my," Reina said, as she bustled up and took Katie's arm. "Looks like we don't need to worry about you two getting along."

Zayn watched as Reina and Serge led Katie away, wondering why she'd decided to kiss him. He didn't understand human females any better than any other type of female. Maybe they changed their minds quickly, or maybe that was a common to say goodbye.

He touched a finger to his lip. He knew he didn't deserve her, but he wanted her more than he'd ever wanted anything.

Chapter Twelve

Katie walked between the two aliens as they chattered away, but her mind was back with Zayn and that kiss. She put a hand to her lips, thinking they must be bruised. She knew she had nothing to complain about. She was the one who'd kissed him, after all. He'd just responded, but what a response.

Her body tingled as she thought back to how he'd reacted, his mouth ravishing hers. She was grateful for Reina's grip on her elbow, since her legs still felt wobbly. She licked her lips and smiled. How had he tasted like doughnuts?

She'd never intended for it to be such a passionate kiss. Her plan had been to put on a good show for the two aliens who were escorting her. She needed to convince them she was all in with the tribute bride thing, if she was going to get the information she needed and get off the station.

As Reina prattled on beside her, Katie realized it had worked. Neither one of them doubted that she was into Zayn. Hell, even she believed it.

Her stomach dropped as they descended in the inclinator, and she clutched Reina for balance as they came to a stop at the promenade level and the doors swished open. It was another perfect day on the idealized space station: water burbled in the fountain, a slight breeze rustled the fabric awnings over the shop entrances, and the scent of coffee hung in the air.

Katie breathed in. "Is there a Starbucks, or am I imagining the smell of Sumatra?" Knowing how many Starbucks there were in LA, she wouldn't have been surprised if they'd put a franchise on an alien space station behind Saturn.

"Starbucks?" Reina twisted her hands. "I'm afraid not, but we do have a lovely shop next to the bridal salon that offers liquid stimulants."

Serge tugged her forward. "There's no time for that. We're going to be late."

Katie stopped in her tracks and folded her arms across her chest, staring down the shorter man.

He threw his hands in the air. "Have it your way, but don't look at me when Monti and Randi give you the stink eye for being late."

She quirked her lips to the side. "Stink eye?"

"His hobby is learning colorful Earth phrases from his brides," Reina said.

"Come on," Serge hurried forward. "Don't just stand there like two bumps on a log."

"I take it some of his brides have been from the South," Katie said, as they followed him toward the smell of freshly brewed coffee.

The glass-fronted shop they entered looked remarkably like a coffee shop on Earth, with rich wood furniture and a long, slate counter. It smelled like a coffee shop, too, the delicious aroma perking Katie up just from the smell. Chalkboard signs hung overhead with drinks listed. As she looked up, designs swirled around the white lettering as if an invisible hand was drawing flowers and leaves along the border.

"Cool, isn't it?" A strikingly pretty African-American woman asked, also staring up at the sign.

"Hey, Katie," Mandy said, leaning over the other woman and giving Katie a finger wave. "This is Bridget. Another tribute bride." She giggled. "Obviously."

"Do you mind?" Serge asked. "We're in a terrible rush."

Bridget held up her hands. "Don't let us stop you." She dropped her voice as Serge strode forward. "We know how crazy Serge can get when he's in full wedding planning mode."

Mandy reached over and squeezed her arm. "If you need a break, let us know."

Katie smiled, but wasn't sure she'd completely forgiven Mandy for being the reason she was in this mess. Of course, if she got her story, it would end up being the best thing that had ever happened to her. That is, if she could also prove to the world she wasn't insane.

"One thing you should know about the coffee here," Bridget said. "It smells right and tastes right, but it's not actually coffee."

Katie felt her shoulders deflate. "What do you mean? What is it?"

"The Drexians have their own version," Mandy said. "It's supposed to be healthy and have a bunch of protein, so don't be surprised when you aren't hungry after one cup."

"Unfortunately, it has a lot more calories than our coffee, so go easy unless you want Monti and Randi letting out your dress the day of the wedding," Bridget added.

Katie frowned. Of course, there was a catch. Healthy, protein-packed coffee couldn't be diet food. Not that she believed in diets.

A blonde entered the shop behind them, and the bell over the door tinkled. She had shoulder-length hair and wore almost no makeup. "Sorry I'm late."

Mandy put an arm around the woman's shoulders. "We were about to order without you, Trista."

The lights in the shop surged brighter for a moment, then returned to normal, and she saw the three tribute brides exchange a glance.

"More glitches on the station?" Katie asked. "Zayn told me about it."

Mandy grinned and whispered to Bridget and Trista, "Zayn is her match."

"Yeah. We figured," Bridget said.

"The glitches are nothing." Mandy gave Bridget a withering look. "Dorn says it's normal, since they're having to repair all the damage and upgrade the station's defenses."

Bridget glanced outside the shop. "It's happening more than it did right after the attack."

Reina shushed them. "Let's not talk about that, ladies. It's bad luck."

"What's bad luck?" Serge asked, as he returned, holding a paper cup and handing it to Katie.

"Nothing," all five women said.

Serge narrowed his eyes at them. "Why do I feel like I'm on the wrong side of a conspiracy?"

———

KATIE TOOK a drink of her mocha, swirling the dregs around the bottom of the cup to get one more decent sip.

"Enough of that." Serge snatched the paper cup from her hands and pushed her to the round platform.

Katie gathered the tulle skirt in her arms and stepped up, holding her arms out, as the platform lifted off the ground and began turning in mid-air.

"I think I'm going to cry," Reina said, watching Katie twirl in front of the three mirrors. Instrumental theme songs from 80s romcoms played in the background, but not loud enough to mask the Vexling's sniffling.

Serge handed the blue-haired woman a hot-pink handkerchief. "Is this the one?"

Katie ran her fingers down the ivory lace column and glanced at her own reflection. After an hour of trying on wedding gowns, she'd returned to the first dress she'd put on—a form-fitting lace gown with long sleeves, a deep V-neckline, and a swish of a train. "It is pretty."

She glimpsed the pile of rejected dresses through the open door of the dressing room. Mostly frilly confections with skirts that swallowed her, and shiny fabrics that made her eyes hurt, she'd suspected the aliens had raided a David's Bridal sample sale. In the 80s. Not that she didn't appreciate good vintage, but most of the dresses weren't old enough to be vintage, or current enough to be stylish. The simple dress she had on was the only one that hadn't made her cringe.

"Wait." One of the dress designers rushed up holding a net veil over his head. "You won't know until you see the full effect."

He winked at her in the mirror, the gold eyeliner that matched his gold hair flashing in the light from the crystal chandelier. "No woman looks like a bride until she has the veil."

"You're forgetting the tiara, Randi," the other dress designer said, the sparkling crown of rhinestones nearly as flashy as his silver hair and bedazzled eyelashes.

The space station's resident dress designers, Monti and Randi— both with an 'i' they'd told her—wore matching black Nehru jackets that reached their thighs and hadn't seemed the least bit deterred when she'd rejected dress after dress.

"At least she's not throwing things at us," Monti had muttered under his breath to Serge when she'd wrinkled her nose at a ball gown with hearts embroidered on the hem.

The pink bubbly Serge had thrust into her hand had helped, and after a few sips, the dresses hadn't seemed so bad. The buzz had made it harder for her to remember all the details though. Katie had to remind herself why she was going along with the ridiculous scheme. She needed to gather as much information as she could about the space station for her exposé.

She eyed the two aliens fussing over her. They definitely weren't human, although from what she could gather, they weren't Drexian, either. The station was filled with aliens with skin tones ranging from blue to green to purple and with curious features like tails, horns, and even tusks. And in the case of Monti and Randi, metallic hair.

She'd been able to determine that Drexians were all big, muscular guys who looked like they had the world's most perfect bronze tan. And they had bumps down their spine that got hard when, well, when they got hard. Her skin warmed as she thought about Zayn standing shirtless on the balcony, the moonlight silhouetting his wide back and the bulges of his arms as he braced himself on the railing. She wondered what his bumps would feel like, and imagined brushing her fingers down his back.

"You're as red as your hair, sweetie," Monti said, narrowing his eyes at her. "I know it's not the tiara that's getting you all hot and bothered."

Katie gave a small shake of her head. "It's nothing."

"Mmm-hmm." He didn't sound convinced, as he swept her hair back and pinned it up under the crown. Standing back, he crossed his arms and looked her up and down before smiling.

Reina choked back a sob and blew her nose into Serge's handkerchief. "It's perfect."

Katie eyed herself in the mirror. She wasn't so sure. The woman looking back at her seemed like a stranger, with her hair pulled up high beneath the sparkly tiara, and a long cascade of tulle spilling around her shoulders and down her back. The lace hugged her curves, and dipped low to reveal the swell of her cleavage. It made her feel sexier than she ever had before, but she'd never thought of herself as sexy. She wondered what Zayn would think if he saw her in the dress, then she pushed that thought out of her mind. She was here for a story, not to get married. Not really. If all went according to plan, she'd be long gone before the day rolled around when she'd have to wear this.

"Well?" Serge asked, waving away Reina and making a face as she tried to return his handkerchief to him.

"Sure," Katie said with a shrug. "Let's go with the dress, but not the tiara."

Monti's shoulders sagged, and Randi sighed. Before either of them could complain, Serge waved a hand over his head. "We're done here."

Reina bustled her back into the dressing room and out of the dress. As they were leaving the salon, Katie tried to catalog the details in her mind. Unfortunately, it looked like a typical high-end bridal salon on Earth. Plush, cream carpeting, racks of silk and satin dresses, an arrangement of fragrant, white lilies by the glass doors. Aside from the two designers, who would have stood out even in LA, and the levitating platform, there was little about the place that would make you think you were on an alien space station.

Katie reminded herself that was the whole point. They'd gone to a lot of trouble to create a place where Earth women would feel at home. As she stepped outside the shop and onto the shimmering cobblestones of the promenade square, she couldn't help feeling that they'd accomplished their goal. Unless she looked up to the domed ceiling of the towering atrium that looked out into space, she could convince herself she was walking around Beverly Hills.

But I'm not, she reminded herself. *I'm on an alien space station that no one knows about. Not yet, at least.*

Serge took her by the elbow as he glanced down at a portable device that flashed a few unfamiliar symbols. "I was able to get us in to see the music specialist."

"You're going to love him," Reina said, putting a hand to her throat. "He's from your home."

"Los Angeles?" Katie asked.

Serge shook his head. "Earth. I think he lived in some place you call Ten Easy."

Katie looked down at Serge, his spiky purple hair unmoving as they hurried down the sidewalk. "Do you mean Tennessee? Like the state?"

"That's what I said." Serge didn't slow as they dodged a blonde walking with a Vexling who looked a lot like Reina.

"I thought you only brought women from Earth up here," Katie said.

"There have been select occasions when well-known Earthlings have wanted to escape their celebrity," Serge said. "We bring them up here, and they can live out their lives in peace."

"Are you telling me you have a station full of missing celebrities?" Katie's paparazzi antennae pricked.

"There aren't that many," Reina said. "Just the ones who don't mind being a part of the tribute bride program in some way."

"So this guy is a celebrity? Was he a famous singer or DJ?" Katie asked, taking one step for every two of Serge's.

Serge sucked in his breath. "DJ? Whatever you do, don't call him a DJ." He paused in front of a brick storefront with a pair of white columns. "We're very lucky to have him, and he doesn't do just *any* wedding." He dropped his voice as if someone was listening. "And he isn't getting any younger."

"Then what do I call him?" Katie asked.

"He's much more humble than you'd expect for one of your kings," Reina said, her gray cheeks filling with color. "He's quite charming."

"King?" Katie said, feeling her pulse begin the quicken. It couldn't be.

Serge rolled his large eyes and pointed a finger at Reina. "No simpering. You would have thought you were one of his hysterical groupies, the way you acted last time."

Reina's cheeks went from pink to red, and she frowned at Serge. As she wrapped her fingers around the brass doorknob, an alarm began wailing and blue lights flashed overhead.

Chapter Thirteen

Zayn heard the alarm and bolted upright, his head aching. He'd only crawled into bed after Katie had left with Serge and Reina to go on wedding appointments. It took a moment for everything to come back to him, and for him to remember that he wasn't in an alien prison.

His heart pounded while he got his bearings, and he nearly fell out of the bed as he kicked off the sheets. He quickly scanned the room. Nothing burning or visibly malfunctioning. That was good. The wailing seemed to be coming from the hall, so he opened the door and sniffed. Again, no smoke. He noticed people emerging from other suites, so he went back inside and dug through the dresser drawers until he found a shirt that wasn't intended for a human female.

Pulling it on, he left the suite and jogged down to the inclinator. If there was no fire, the station must be under attack, he thought. He felt the floor tremble as the lights blinked off and on, and a sharp pain jabbed into his temple. He clutched the side of his head, but the pain went away as quickly as it had appeared. The doctors had warned him he might experience residual pain from his torture.

"Nothing I can't handle," he told himself as he stepped into the sleek inclinator car, drumming his fingers against his leg. The usual piped-in music and lavender uplighting was gone, no doubt a result of the power fluctuations.

Zayn hoped Katie was safe, although he couldn't remember where they said she'd be going. Memories of the kiss she'd given him before she left made his cock swell, and he readjusted himself. He'd been surprised she'd kissed him, but even more surprised by his body's reaction. He couldn't blame his overpowering desire on being asleep this time. Even if his mind knew he didn't deserve her, his body clearly had different ideas. He fisted his hands. He'd just have to be stronger. He'd survived being tortured by the Kronock, hadn't he?

He barely refrained from laughing out loud. He'd almost rather be back in a Kronock cell, than have to resist his tribute bride. He thought of her wavy, red hair spilling across the pillow and felt his chest tighten. Her body had been so soft and warm beneath his. Even though he knew he didn't deserve her, he couldn't help thinking of her as his to protect. The idea of her being in danger made his stomach tighten into a hard ball.

Think, he told himself. Where would she be? Dress shopping, that was it. He brushed a finger across the directional panel to send him to the promenade level and felt the compartment drop. Even though he hadn't done more than glance at the centerpiece of the station, he knew the shops were there. He also knew that with its open, soaring ceiling, it would be most vulnerable to attacks.

When he reached the promenade level, he scanned the area for a flash of her hair. The shops appeared to be empty, and no one strolled by the fountain, although water still splashed down into the round pool from the stone figure. From what he'd seen of Serge, he felt sure Katie had been taken to a safe location. The station went dark and silent, then jerked as the lights came back on.

Zayn spun on his heel and returned to the inclinator. He wanted to get to the top level before the station lost power again, and held his breathe as he surged upward. Reaching the top, he exited and strode to the bridge without slowing, his eyes searching for the captain.

The man spotted him and exchanged a look with the Drexian he was huddled in conversation with before walking over to him. "You shouldn't be here."

Zayn saluted the captain and the Drexian warrior who'd walked over with him. "What's going on? Are we under attack?"

The captain turned to the other man. "The warrior who recently escaped the Kronock."

"I know of your escape." The uniformed warrior gave him a brisk chest salute even though Zayn was not in uniform. "Commander Dorn."

"Inferno Force?" Zayn asked, recognizing the name instantly and the notorious fleet he commanded. A flick of his eyes to the insignia on the Drexian's uniform confirmed it.

Dorn frowned. "Not at the moment. I came to the Boat to take a bride and have yet to return to battle."

Zayn felt a kinship with the warrior that went beyond shared Drexian blood. From the restless look in his eyes, he knew this man understood what it felt like to be kept from what he did best.

Zayn looked out the wide wall of windows into space and saw nothing but stars. "When the station shook, I thought the enemy had brought the battle to us."

The captain gave a single shake of his head as the dim lights flickered on the bridge. "We're experiencing some odd malfunctions."

Zayn allowed himself to take a normal breath. "So it's not the Kronock?"

Dorn rocked back on his heels. "We pushed them back to the outskirts of the galaxy, but the station still hasn't fully recovered from their initial attack."

Zayn felt his impatience rise. "They'll return."

"And we'll keep repelling them. Like we have for years," Dorn said, then tilted his head at him. "Shouldn't you be with your mate?"

"She's out doing wedding tasks," Zayn said, feeling embarrassed that he didn't know exactly where she was. "I believe the Gatazoid took her someplace safe."

Dorn clapped a hand on his shoulder. "You know, I was in the same position you're in just a few weeks ago. I understand what you're going through."

Zayn doubted the confident warrior understood what it was like to come back after living in a cell and being tortured daily.

"The last thing I wanted was to be paired off with some human female," Dorn continued. "I wanted to get back to my ship and battle my enemy. I fought the match as hard as I could."

"Really?" Maybe he did understand.

"Until I realized resisting was pointless. Accepting a human match was part of my duty as a Drexian, and it's part of yours, too." Dorn nudged him. "The human females have many attributes you may not be aware of yet, and they're not as fragile as they look."

Zayn felt blood rush to his face as he recalled the look on Katie's face when he'd pinned her down. Maybe not, but he knew from experience how easily he could overpower her.

"I'd be of better use to the Empire if I could be reassigned to a fighting unit," he said. "The medical team gave me a clean bill of health. I'm ready to go back and fight."

Dorn grinned. "I'm with you, brother, but the place we need to defend most is here. The Kronock would love to get their hands on this station."

"Then let me help defend it," Zayn argued. "I'm a good pilot and a better fighter."

The controls flickered on the consoles and Zayn put a hand to his head, wincing from the jolt of pain.

Dorn studied him. "You sure you're okay?"

"It's nothing," he said, but he knew from the look on the other warrior's face that he'd blown it.

"Listen." Dorn took him by the elbow and steered him toward the door. "These are just glitches in the power systems. I promise if we get another visit by the Kronock, I'll draft you back into service. I can tell you one thing, however. As a commander, I'd rather have a fully rested and recovered warrior, than one who returned to action too soon."

Zayn cast a wistful look around the sparse, metal interior of the bridge, envious of the Drexians manning their stations. His fingers twitched at his side, itching to move across a console again and hold a weapon

"Now what you should really be concerned about is what that crazy little wedding planner is up to. If you're not careful, you'll end up standing in something called a 'butterfly garden' trying to locate your testicles." Dorn rubbed a hand over his forehead. "Trust me on this one."

Zayn managed to smile as he left the bridge and made his way back through the space station. Maybe Dorn was right and he should focus on getting fully recuperated. If High Command knew he was still having pain, not to mention night terrors, they would never give him another assignment again. Luckily, only Katie knew how bad his dreams were, and somehow he trusted her not to say anything.

He scolded himself for thinking of her again. Why was it so hard to push a single human female from his thoughts?

Chapter Fourteen

"This is an emergency bunker?" Katie asked, taking in the elaborately decorated room Reina had whisked her to underneath the bridal salon.

"More like our man cave," Monti said with a swish of his wrist as Randi nodded.

Katie had seen man caves before, masculine basements with black-leather furniture and massive flat screens. This long narrow room looked more like a nightclub. Low, white poufs dotted the room with equally low and round tables. A curved, white-leather bar sat at the far end, surrounded by metallic stools that appeared to be hovering in mid-air, and pale-blue light glowed from behind the milky-white walls.

"Who wants a drink while we wait for the 'all clear?'" Randi swept behind the bar and began to place tall glass cylinders in front of him.

The walls changed from blue to pink as Katie hopped on one of the stools and spun around on the floating seat. "I could go for a drink. You don't happen to have snacks down here, do you?"

Monti bustled behind the bar, disappearing from view. His shiny, silver hair reappeared followed by the rest of him, and he held out a clear tray with what looked like a row of cookies.

Katie's stomach growled. She'd had a few bites of the Drexian version of a doughnut before she'd gotten in the shower, and she'd finished the protein-packed coffee, but she was still hungry. "Are those chocolate chip?"

Monti pushed the tray toward her, nodding. "They're something-chip."

Katie picked up a cookie and eyed it with suspicion. "Something-chip" wasn't reassuring. She took a tiny bite from the edge. It tasted like chocolate chip, with only a hint of smoky flavor when she swallowed. It was better than nothing, she reasoned, as she took a bigger bite.

"Okay, this should be everyone," Serge said, as he navigated the spiral stairs in his platform shoes with a group of people behind him.

Katie recognized Bridget, Mandy, and Trista.

"Are you getting sick of us yet?" Mandy asked, laughing as the three women joined Katie at the bar. She motioned to the blonde. "I don't think we introduced you properly before. This is Trista. She was one of the original three who were on 'The Dating Game' when we got here."

Katie swallowed and brushed crumbs off her lips. "The Dating Game?"

"It's a long story," Trista said.

Bridget dropped her voice. "And one that includes Mandy demanding a mate with a huge—"

Mandy swatted at her as her cheeks flooded with color. "I was provoked!"

Trista and Bridget both shook their heads and laughed.

"Fine," Mandy said, finally laughing as well. "I was freaked out and wanted to shock everyone. That was before I knew they were aliens and we were on a space station."

"I'm still not clear why there was a dating game involved," Katie said.

"It was how they used to match up Drexians and humans," Trista said. "I'm pretty sure our game was the last time they did that, though."

Bridget nodded. "They finally realized how outdated it was."

Katie remembered Mandy saying something about all of this when they'd first met, but since she'd also revealed that they were on a space station behind Saturn, the dating game part of the story hadn't stuck out. "So you three were the contestants?"

Bridget grinned. "But Mandy sweet-talked them into picking her."

Mandy put both hands on her hips. "Ha-ha." She spotted the tray of cookies Monti had placed on the top of the bar. "Are those chocolate chip?"

"Kind of," Katie said. She took another nibble, herself. "So I never asked. How did we all get up here? Transporter beams?"

"The Drexians can fly at light speed, so the journey from Earth to here doesn't take long." Mandy looked to Reina for confirmation. "About an hour and a half on one of the transport ships, right?"

Reina nodded. "You would have been out during that time."

"And no satellites from Earth pick up on a ship shooting off the surface at light speed?" Katie asked.

"They have pretty cool cloaking technology," Bridget said. "All their ships have these sweet black hulls which are actually made of high-tech stealth panels."

Katie swung her feet from the barstool. "I'm kind of sorry I slept through the trip."

"You weren't sleeping," Reina said. "An onboard medical team would have checked you over, given you the necessary inoculations for life in space and among other species, and implanted an auditory universal translator so you can understand the rest of us, as well as a tracker."

"A what?" Katie asked, noticing Serge giving the Vexling a sharp elbow to the leg.

"It's standard," Serge said. "We all have them for security purposes."

"You GPSed us?" Mandy asked, her mouth agape.

Serge smoothed his wide lapels. "Like I said, it's standard."

Even if it was standard, Katie could tell the other women had no idea about it. She guessed it wasn't something the Drexians announced. Clearly, even aliens who abducted their brides knew implanting trackers in them was creepy. It would, however, make a great part of her story.

Monti clapped his hands to get their attention. "We designed this bunker in case we ever needed to survive here, so we've got all the essentials."

"Cocktails, anyone?" Randi motioned to the now-filled glasses and lifted one himself, the peach-hued contents sloshing over the rim.

Serge gave both designers a severe look. "Cocktails are not survival essentials."

"Maybe not to you," Monti mumbled from behind the rim of his glass.

Katie eyed the drinks. "I feel like it's early to be drinking. Isn't it still morning?"

"Don't worry, sweetie," Randi pushed a glass toward her and winked, his gold eyeliner glinting at her. "These are mild. No Palaxian Pleasure Tonic, I promise."

Katie wished she could be taking notes. Was she going to remember all this? She repeated the items in her mind: Palaxian Pleasure Tonic, a fake game show to match Drexians with brides, floating barstools. These were the details that would make her story authentic.

"Too bad," Mandy said. "You haven't lived until you've tried Palaxian Pleasure Tonic."

"I don't know about that," Trista said. "I haven't tried it."

"That's because your mate hasn't arrived yet," Mandy told her, then turned to Katie. "Her Drexian is involved in a battle far away from here, so she hasn't even met him yet."

"It's okay," Trista said. "I'm not in any rush."

Katie noticed her quivering voice. Terrified, was probably more like it. "So you're just hanging out until he gets here?"

Trista nodded. "At first, I didn't want to leave my room. This whole thing was so overwhelming. I'd never even left Iowa before coming here."

Katie knew she couldn't use real names in her story, but Trista would make a great opening for her exposé. The girl from Iowa who'd never left her home state before being abducted by aliens? That was pure gold.

"What made you come around?" Katie asked.

"Well, I really didn't want to go back to Iowa." Her face darkened. "I know it isn't an option anyway, but a big part of me is glad to be out of there. I don't know if I would have had the courage to get out on my own."

Katie watched the woman's expression change as she seemed to give herself a mental shake. "So you're happy here?"

Trista glanced at the other women, who were chatting with Randi and Monti. "Happier. Bridget and Mandy have been great about getting me out of my shell." She rolled her eyes. "They drag me everywhere."

Bridget looped an arm around Trista's waist. "Since my husband is also away on a mission, I have someone to commiserate with."

Mandy winked at Katie. "The difference is Bridget knows what she's missing with Kax gone. Trista has no idea what she's in for."

If that was meant to comfort the Midwestern woman, the startled look on Trista's face told Katie it hadn't worked. For a moment, Katie wondered what would happen to everyone on the station if she exposed their secrets. Would they have to shut down? She liked Reina and Serge, and hated the idea of putting them out of a job. Then again, a story of this magnitude couldn't be kept from people. It was her duty to let Earth know what was going on, wasn't it?

"So what about your guy, Katie?" Bridget asked, sweeping her black hair back away from her face.

"Zayn?" Katie's heart rate increased just thinking of him. "He's fine."

"He sure is," Monti said, leaning over the bar.

"When did you see him?" Katie asked.

"We get photos of the brides and their Drexian warriors before every appointment," Randi said. "Helps us get an idea of what would look good."

"So?" Mandy prodded. "Tell us about him. He's Drexian, so we know he's big and built. What else?"

Katie's pulse quickened as she shifted on the levitating stool. "I really just met him." No way was she going to tell anyone what had happened between them, or that he had nightmares about his last battle. Even mentioning his headaches seemed disloyal, although she wasn't sure why she felt loyalty to him when she'd rarely been loyal to anyone her entire life. There was something about him she felt like she needed to protect. It was not a sensation she enjoyed.

"That's not the way it looked from your goodbye kiss this morning," Reina said.

Mandy's eyebrows popped up. "That's a good sign."

Katie reminded herself that she was supposed to be convincing everyone that she was all-in on the tribute bride thing. She gave what she hoped was a provocative smile. "Like you said, he is hot."

Suddenly, the lights in the walls went dark, and the floating bar stool fell almost to the floor, before stopping and hovering an inch or two above. The women screamed as glasses went flying along with peach liquid. Mandy fell off her stool, and Katie caught herself with her free hand before rolling onto the shiny, white floor.

"Is it just me, or are those getting worse?" Bridget asked, as she helped Mandy up.

Reina clutched her throat. "You don't think it's another attack, do you?" She turned to Serge. "Should we get the brides to an escape pod?"

"This is probably just more issues from the last attack," Serge said as he held onto the bar for support. "We stay down here until we get orders to evacuate."

Katie couldn't help thinking about Zayn and the pains he got that seemed to be triggered by the power fluctuations. This couldn't be helping. Her mind went to the big warrior and the feel of his arms wrapped around her. She hoped he was okay.

As she thought more about him, she knew that he was the Drexian she should be questioning. He'd survived being taken prisoner by aliens, and knew what the species hoping to invade Earth was really like. If her story was going to be more than a profile of fancy space station, the hot alien in her room was the source she needed. She just hoped she wasn't getting in too deep with him already.

"Um, Katie?" Trista nudged her in the side. "I think you have a visitor."

Katie followed the woman's gaze to the spiral stairs and the Drexian warrior coming down it wearing nothing but drawstring pants and a T-shirt that showed every rock-hard curve of his muscles. "Zayn?"

Chapter Fifteen

Zayn scanned the group of women and aliens sitting on hovering barstools and drinking colorful cocktails. He'd scoured the promenade until one of the waiters at the bakery had told him about the bunker beneath the bridal salon, but this chic space was not what he'd expected.

"Are you okay?" he asked as Katie hurried over to him.

The other women—he recognized one as the tribute bride who'd greeted Katie in their suite and assumed the rest were tributes, as well—smiled and gave each other knowing looks. An alien with silver hair raised a cocktail and an eyebrow in salute.

"I'm fine." She reached out and touched his hand. "Are you?"

He tentatively brushed a curl off her forehead. "Just worried about you."

She blushed as everyone in the room sighed or made noises of approval. "Is everything back to normal up top?"

He took her hand in his. "I'm here to escort you, in case there are more power fluctuations."

"Escort her where?" Serge piped up. "We still have an appointment to select music."

Zayn saw the Vexling named Reina elbow Serge in the ribs, then whisper something he couldn't quite make out.

"You're right, Reina," he said, then raised his voice so it carried across the room. "We can always reschedule if you two have better things to do."

Zayn looked down and noticed that Katie's cheeks were a patch-work of pink. He got the feeling she disliked being the center of attention, especially if the attention speculated on their mating. He rubbed one thumb across the back of her hand. "We don't have to go back to our suite. There are other things on the station to see."

She grinned up at him, the pink of her cheeks fading. "Let's go."

The other tributes waved and called out farewells, as he led her up the stairs and through the bridal shop. He ducked to avoid hitting his head on the glittering chandelier as they exited onto the promenade.

"So, what should we see?" Katie asked once they were standing across from the burbling fountain.

He shifted from one foot to the other, still holding her by the hand. "To be honest, I don't know much about this station. I only said that so you'd come with me."

She laughed. "Tricky, but I'm glad you did it. I was getting over-whelmed by all the tribute bride talk."

"I thought you'd enjoy spending time with other humans." He started walking toward the inclinator at the end of the shimmering stone walkway, pulling her with him.

"It's not that I don't like talking to them. They're perfectly nice. Nicer than most people I knew on Earth, actually. It's just that I'm not used to the whole 'girl talk' thing."

He tilted his head at her. "I've lived most of my life surrounded by warriors, so I would be unfamiliar with 'girl talk,' as well. I've actually spent very little time talking to females."

"For a newbie, you're not bad," Katie said.

He tightened his grip on her hand, enjoying the warmth and how small it felt encased in his. "Thank you. You're much easier to talk with than the Cressidian pleasurers."

"Cressidian pleasurers?" she asked as they stepped into an empty inclinator compartment.

Zayn nodded. "They're known to be the most enjoyable pleasurers because of their empathic abilities, but I find you much more intriguing."

She stared up at him, as the inclinator surged up. "Did you just say I'm easier to talk to than a hooker?"

"It's a very high compliment," he said, noting that her eyebrows had popped up.

"Okay." The corner of her mouth twitched. "I'll take it as a compliment then. Just don't expect me to do the same tricks these Cressidians do. I'm not into swinging from chandeliers."

Now *his* eyebrows went up. "Is that a mating ritual on Earth?"

She giggled. "No, it's more of an expression." She faced forward as the inclinator rotated. "Now where are we going?"

"I know that each of the holographic wings has its own gathering spot. Instead of going to the one on our wing, I thought we could try out one of the other wings."

"So cocktails in a different setting?" she asked. "I love that idea. After dress shopping and hiding in an underground bunker, I could use a drink."

The inclinator door swished open and a blast of cold air greeted them, making Zayn very aware of how thin his clothing was.

Katie shivered and rubbed one hand on her bare arm. "Which wing is this? The Himalayas?"

Zayn didn't know what that meant, but he did remember the name he'd been told. "The Swiss Alps. The Après Ski bar is supposed to be very charming."

"Then let's find it fast." Katie tugged him forward down the wooden plank walkway that was dusted with a snow. More snow fell from above, and Zayn flinched as it hit his skin.

Within a few meters, the walkway forked in two, and he spotted a wooden building to the left with a peaked roof covered in white. Wide windows seemed to flicker from within, and smoke curled up from a chimney. They ran the rest of the way, bursting through the doors and causing the few people inside to turn abruptly.

"Sorry," Katie said, wiping her arms and giving a wave to a couple at the long bar who'd looked up.

Zayn stared at the snow on his arms as it rapidly melted and dripped onto the polished wood floors. "I've heard of snow, but I've never experienced it before."

"Really?" she asked, as he led her to a pair of brown oversized chairs angled in front of a crackling fireplace. "I don't have a lot of experience with it, either, but do they not have snow on your home world?"

"I don't know. I don't have any memory of the Drexian home world. I grew up on outposts all over the galaxy, but none of them had snow." He looked out the window to where it fell in a soft curtain. "It's pretty."

"Especially when you're inside by a fire."

Zayn looked over to where the firelight warmed her skin and made her hair look even more like a halo of flames. The brief run had made her cheeks pink and her eyes bright. All the blood in his body rushed south, and his cock stirred. He crossed his arms over his lap. The last thing he wanted to do after last night was scare her with a huge erection.

A Gatazoid female hurried over, depositing two steaming mugs on the round table in front of them. "House specialty. Hot Buttered Rump."

"Did she say rump?" Katie asked, picking up her mug of light brown liquid and blowing on it.

Zayn plucked the dried padwump stirrer out of his drink. "Yes, she did."

Katie took a sip. "It's not bad. A little sweet, but with a kick."

Zayn knew there was some sort of alcohol in the drink, but as he took a long gulp, he couldn't determine what kind. As long as it wasn't Noovian whiskey, he'd be fine.

Katie took another drink, sinking back in her chair. "I'm feeling more relaxed already. Thanks for saving me from an afternoon of wedding planning."

"Saving you is my job," he said, the cocktail warming him and making his fingers buzz.

She smiled at him over the rim of her mug. "I'm still not used to the idea of us being assigned to each other. What if a match doesn't work out? What if you hated me?"

"Not possible. How could I hate you? You're the most perfect female I've ever seen."

He wondered why he'd confessed that, and glanced at his now-empty mug. They wouldn't put Palaxian Pleasure Tonic in these, would they?

"You think I'm perfect?" She narrowed her eyes at him and took another long gulp. "You barely know me. What if I have a horrible temper or a nasty drug habit? What if I was obsessed with watching the shopping network?"

"Are you?" He put his mug down on the table and wiggled his tingling fingers.

"No, but I'm far from perfect. Trust me." She gave her head a small shake. "On second hand, you shouldn't trust me."

"No?" He chuckled. "Are you dangerous?"

She winked at him, setting her own empty mug down. "Deadly."

Standing up, Katie crossed to his chair and settled herself on his lap. She looped her arms around his shoulders and nuzzled her face in his neck. Zayn's body hummed with desire, and his cock hardened as the soft curve of her ass pressed against it.

"I think our drinks may have had Palaxian Pleasure Tonic in them," he said, trying to slow his own rapid breathing.

"The other tributes mentioned that," Katie said, her words slurred. "They said it's supposed to be really good."

His muddled mind weighed the options of letting her continue to nibble on his neck and telling her the truth. "It might make you do something you will later regret," he finally said.

"I won't regret anything I do to you," she whispered, running a hand down his chest. "Just touching you makes me feel like I'm on fire."

"That's the pleasure tonic," he said, now noticing other couples with similarly empty mugs locked in embraces around the room.

She shook her head. "I've been wanting to touch you since the first time I saw you, but I'm normally too shy."

"Katie." He wrapped his arms around her and pulled her closer to him. "I'm all yours. You can touch me anyway you want."

"Tempting," she said, raising her head and kissing him gently.

Zayn sank into the kiss, moaning as her tongue parted his lips, and he tasted the lingering sweetness of the drink. His cock was throbbing now, and he arched up so that it ground against her.

Katie gasped and pulled away, glancing down at his lap. "It feels even bigger than it looks." She bit the corner of her lower lip. "I've never had one that big."

"I promise I won't hurt you," he said, tracing a finger along her jaw.

"I know you won't hurt me." She stroked a hand down his cheek. "How is it that I trust you when I barely know you?"

"The same reason my heart clenches every time I look at you."

She giggled. "Are you saying you believe in fate? Isn't that a bit superstitious for a super advanced alien?"

"I only know what I feel when I look at you," he said. "That you are mine to protect and cherish. Forever."

Katie blinked a few times. "No guy has ever said anything like that to me."

"They were the wrong guys."

"No kidding," she said, arching a brow and wiggling her hips on his cock. "And none of them had anything close to this."

He brushed a curl off her forehead. "When we are mated, I'll be very gentle."

Katie gave him a mischievous grin. "Too bad." She leaned over so her lips were next to his ear. "I like it hard."

Zayn fought to keep himself from throwing her to the rug and claiming her right there in front of the fire, reminding himself that it was the pleasure tonic talking. He knew *his* feelings were real, even if his lips were looser than he'd like them to be, but he could not act upon her lowered inhibitions. He wanted nothing more than to take her slow and savor every sensation, but not when she was drunk on pleasure tonic.

"Zayn?" Katie asked, her sultry tone snapping him out of his thoughts. "I think you should take me back to our suite."

Grek.

Chapter Sixteen

"Neither of you happen to have a pair of sunglasses on you, do you?" Katie asked, shielding her eyes as they stepped off the inclinator and onto the promenade. Usually, she thought the shimmery cobblestones were pretty, but today they seemed to be glaring up at her.

"Sunglasses?" Reina gave a high-pitched giggle. "Why would we need sunglasses when we're so far from the sun?"

The Vexling's chirpy voice made Katie's head pound even more. "No reason."

"Would it have to do with the fact that you and Zayn were spotted drinking in the Swiss Chalet?" Serge asked, narrowing his eyes at her.

"What? No." Katie's cheeks warmed. "How did you know that?"

Serge bustled forward, then stopped and looked back over his shoulders. "There's little that happens with my tribute brides that I don't know about, darling."

Katie hoped he didn't know everything that happened last night, or everything she said. The one thing she could be glad about was that she and Zayn had fallen asleep almost as soon as they'd reached their suite. She remembered trying to do a semblance of a strip tease before realizing he was snoring, and then curling up next to him.

"The drinks they serve there are way stronger than any hot toddy I've had on Earth," she said. "I don't know what they put in them, but they pack a punch."

"Palaxian Pleasure Tonic," Serge said, with a wave of his hand.

"That's right. Zayn mentioned something about that possibly being in the drinks." Bits of the evening came back to her, and she hoped her face didn't show her embarrassment at the memories. Had she really told him she'd never felt a cock as large as his. She almost groaned out loud. Way to play it cool, Katie. She knew her plan was to butter him up to get information, but she wasn't sure if she was ready to butter him up *that* much.

Reina shook her head. "They shouldn't put that in a drink unless they warn you."

"A warning sign would have been nice," Katie agreed, although at the time she'd been perfectly happy to lose some of her inhibitions. If she was being honest with herself, it had felt really good to be in the moment. She'd spent so much of her life working an angle, it had been freeing to not think of any of that.

"Come on, ladies," Serge said from several feet ahead of them. "We've got lots to do today, and you two are walking slower than molasses in winter."

Katie raised an eyebrow, as Reina muttered something about Serge and his Earth sayings.

"Remind me again who we're seeing today," she said, speeding up her pace and marveling at how fast Serge could walk, even though his legs were significantly shorter than hers or Reina's.

Before Serge could answer her, Katie's stomach dropped. Actually, the entire station dropped away as Katie floated off the ground. Serge yelped as he, too, lifted off from the cobblestones. Looking around, Katie saw that everything not secured to the ground was floating. Bistro tables bobbed by and even the water in the fountain was drifting up into the air in an undulating blob.

"It's the station's gravity," Reina cried out, grabbing hold of Katie's ankle from below.

Katie peered down and saw that the willowy alien had one elbow hooked around a lamppost to keep her tethered to the floor. As Serge somersaulted past her, Katie reached for him, clutching one of his wide, green lapels and pulling him closer.

He stared at her from his upside down vantage point. "This is intolerable!"

"These malfunctions are getting more intense," Katie said, remembering when the gravity had flickered off and back on the day before, when they were in the bunker.

She looked up and gulped. The open-air promenade soared at least two hundred feet overhead, and furniture was drifting up toward the clear domed ceiling. Katie cursed under her breath. If Reina hadn't grabbed her, she might be fifty feet in the air by now.

Luckily, it seemed like most people who'd been on the promenade had been able to grab something stationery, but there was lots of shrieking. Most of it coming from Serge.

"I cannot work under these conditions," he said, his voice shrill. "I'm going to be lodging a serious of formal complaints as soon as my feet touch the ground."

"I'm sure they'll get things back to normal soon," Katie told him as she adjusted her grip on his jacket.

He grabbed her hands. "For the love of everything holy, do not let go of me!"

She pressed her lips together to keep from laughing, the absurdity of the situation overtaking her fear. "I promise."

As abruptly as the gravity had disappeared, it suddenly returned. Katie fell to the ground on top of Reina with Serge collapsing in her lap. Tables and chairs crashed around them, and Katie raised her arms over her head to shield herself from anything else that might fall from above. After a few seconds, she looked out from under her arms.

Serge's face was beet-red from hanging upside down and his jacket rumpled from where she'd held on to him. He stood up and brushed himself off, giving both her and Reina a small bow. "It seems I owe both of you a debt of gratitude for not letting me float away like a balloon."

"Anytime," Katie said, although she hoped this would not become a regular occurrence. It would, however, make a great detail for her exposé. She nibbled the corner of her lip as she thought about her article. With all the things happening on the station, it was clear she needed to speed up her timetable. If the Boat was gradually falling apart or breaking down, she didn't want to be here when it finally failed.

She thought of Zayn and felt a twinge. Come on, Katie, she scolded herself. You know you never get emotionally involved with a mark. And no matter how hot he was or how he made her feel, he was her mark. He was also the key to her story.

Tonight, Katie thought. Tonight she'd get what she needed from Zayn. Standing up, she glanced at the furniture that had crashed into the fountain and spotted a Drexian with a bloodied leg. No, she couldn't think about Zayn. She'd get her juicy scoop and get the hell out of here. Before it was too late.

Chapter Seventeen

Zayn was on autopilot as he made his way down the walkway. The power fluctuations had stopped, along with the shooting pains in his head, but he didn't feel any better. Not after drinking Palaxian Pleasure tonic the night before. Luckily, he and Katie had both passed out once they'd reached their bed, not waking until Serge and Reina had arrived and hustled her off to more appointments.

He'd been almost glad for the two aliens' abrupt arrival, since it saved him from the awkward moment when Katie remembered what they'd almost done. He'd seen a flicker of embarrassment in her eyes as Reina had hurried her to dress, and it was a stab to his gut after their closeness the night before. He knew it had been a manufactured intimacy, but he'd never thought pleasure tonic revealed any emotions that weren't already present. It only seemed to release them. He knew he hadn't said anything to her he didn't actually feel, and he held out hope that the same was true of his mate.

Zayn rubbed his aching head. He wasn't up to a session in the gym, but he knew the Drexian's gym also had a pool. A few laps might loosen his muscles, and take his mind off both his nightmares and his new redheaded distraction. The monotony of swimming laps had always helped him clear his mind.

Following the corridors until he reached the training area, he crossed through the expansive gym, with its hovering punching bags and holographic boxing ring, and entered an even larger room with a clear, hexagonal ceiling. The long, rectangular pool stretched from one end to the other with a white deck surrounding it. The floor felt like rubbery pebbles beneath his feet as he kicked off his shoes and crossed to a wall of cubbies, pulling out a standard issue swimsuit.

He was the only one in the room, so he shed his clothes quickly and pulled on the suit, which fit like a tighter version of his boxer briefs. Climbing onto one of the starter blocks, he swung his arms back and forth until they touched behind him. His skin felt tight where it had grown back over his scars, and he watched it pucker when he flexed his forearms. Zayn knew these scars would remain, along with his internal ones.

He dove into the water, feeling the jolt as his body hit the cold, welcoming the cool against his skin as his arms sliced through the water and grateful his family had once been stationed on an outpost near a deep lake. His best memories from his childhood were swimming in that black lake that had been so deep he'd never been able to touch the bottom.

Thinking about growing up made him think about his parents, which made him swim harder. Both Drexian, they had not been members of the elite class. His father had been a grunt and had worked his way up fighting on the oldest ships and being assigned to defend the most remote outposts. Zayn had sworn he'd bring his family honor when he grew up, and earn his own command.

His fingers touched the slick end of the pool and he flipped underwater, kicking hard as he broke the surface. He was glad his parents hadn't lived long enough to witness his disgrace.

How did the High Command not consider his mission a failure? His entire team had been slaughtered. He'd been unable to save even one, and he'd been captured and tortured. He hadn't broken, but he also hadn't been able to save the other Drexian being held with him. In the end, he'd only escaped with his life and the knowledge that the Kronock were creating mutated versions of themselves. Hardly what he'd call a victory, but here he was on the Boat, being rewarded with a tribute bride and being treated like a victor. It didn't feel right, although he did not regret being matched with Katie. She was the only part of this he did not want to give up.

After a few more laps, his shoulders burned and the water no longer felt cool. He pushed through, scissoring his legs harder to propel himself. As he reached for the wall again, a pain shot through his head and made him convulse as if he'd been electrocuted. He squeezed his eyes until the sensation passed and he could raise his head from the water.

Looking around, he expected the lights to go off, but he felt himself being lifted along with the water beneath him. His stomach dropped as he recognized the weightless feel of zero gravity. Shiny, black kick boards levitated over the pool deck and bathing suits rose from the cubicles and hovered in the air. The water surged up and covered the part of his upper body not submerged already.

Zayn tried to push it off his face but it adhered to him as if attached with glue. He forced himself not to breathe in as he thrashed in the undulating water, but the urge to suck in air was instinctive and powerful. His lungs seared as he tried to calm his mind. After surviving seemingly endless torture at the hands of his enemy, he refused to die in a swimming pool because of a gravity malfunction. His chest convulsed as he held his mouth and eyes closed, spots of light dancing across his dark lids.

As quickly as the water had covered him, it dropped away, and the contents of the pool crashed back down, the bathing suits and kick boards dropping to the floor. Water splashed over the edge, soaking the pool deck. Zayn landed where he'd begun and pulled himself over to the side and out, his torso splayed on the bumpy surface and his legs dangling in the water as he sucked in lungfuls of air. He crawled out completely and dropped, his breathing jagged.

These were no normal fluctuations, he thought. Something else was going on. He didn't know what, but he knew the fact that his pains could predict each occurrence was not normal. Either he was going crazy, he'd become a seer of some sort, or…He didn't want to think about the other alternative.

With shaky hands, he changed out of the bathing suit and pulled his clothes over his damp skin. He needed to talk to someone. But who? If he went to the medical bay, they'd hook him up to machines and poke him full of needles. He wasn't sure if he could handle that after being tortured with devices that could have doubled as surgical tools. If he told the captain or the Inferno Force commander, he'd never serve as a warrior again.

He could tell Katie, he thought, as he stumbled out of the pool and through the gym. She already knew about his dreams and his pains. She hadn't told anyone yet, so maybe he could trust her. She was the only person who wouldn't be shocked by his admission, that, he knew for sure.

Zayn was distracted by his thoughts as he walked through the station and entered the Safari wing, not noticing the people he passed or the late-afternoon sun dipping low over the holographic horizon. The doors to his suite swished open, and he was halfway across the room before he saw Katie standing in front of him in a shimmery, black dress that hugged her curves and scooped down low in the front. Her hair spilled loose over her shoulders, and he could see the outline of her nipples beneath the thin fabric.

He tried not to gape, but his mouth fell open before he could stop himself.

"Hungry?" she asked, letting her tongue wet her lower lip and smiling at him.

Chapter Eighteen

K atie pushed her nerves aside as she stood in front of Zayn. He'd been staring at her for a full minute without speaking, and even thought she was pretty sure the open mouth was a signal he liked her dress, it would be nice if he said something. She'd purchased the dress two days before, but now that she stood there in nothing but black silk held in place by the thinnest of straps, she started to second-guess herself.

First of all, she wasn't sure she was even wearing a dress. For all she knew, it could be a fancy slip. The second problem was that she'd never actually set out to seduce someone. Those weren't the types of cons her dad pulled, and even if he had, he wouldn't have used his daughter as bait. The man might have been a grifter, but he never risked her virtue in his schemes.

It's all for the greater good, she reminded herself as she watched Zayn's eyes rake over her body and his pupils dilate. The more she could learn about the Drexians, the tribute brides, and the station they were on, the better her story would be. The people of Earth deserved to know that aliens existed, she reasoned. The women of Earth definitely deserved to know they were being used as payment for the planet's protection. And most of all, they needed to know about the Kronock, especially since the aliens were hell-bent on invading Earth.

"I thought we might have dinner on the balcony," she said, clearing her throat and sweeping a hand to indicate the table for two set up outside with a crisp, white tablecloth and crystal candlesticks.

Zayn dragged his eyes from her and took in the setup, nodding at the levitating silver ice bucket chilling a bottle of wine and the silver domes covering two plates. He looked back at her. "Is this something humans do? Eat outside?"

Katie laughed. "Yeah. I never thought about it, but I guess we do. We spend tons of money on fancy restaurants and huge mansions, and then everyone flocks to the patios." She turned and walked to the table, trying to throw an extra shimmy in her step. "Do you want to eat, or talk about how weird humans are?"

Zayn followed, taking a seat across from her. His eyes went to the bottle in the hovering ice bucket, and he raised an eyebrow. "Palaxian wine?"

Katie shrugged and tried to assume her most innocent face. "Reina said it was the best. Why?"

Reina had also warned her about it, reminding her about the spiked hot toddies from the chalet.

He gave a curt shake of his head as he lifted the bottle and poured. "No reason."

She couldn't help noticing how the muscles of his forearms moved under his scarred flesh. His shirt was short sleeved and tight, stretching across the bulges of his chest and the flat surface of his stomach. It also looked damp, which was odd. Katie was glad she couldn't see any lower as they sat the table, since she knew his drawstring pants were just as thin and revealing as his shirt.

"Cheers," she said, raising her glass once he'd filled both. Her voice sounded artificially cheery in her head, and she made a mental note to tone it down. One of the keys to a good con was appearing natural. She'd never get him to talk if he could sense she was forcing it.

They both drank, and the fizzy wine tickled Katie's throat. He grimaced and put down the glass.

"You don't like it?"

"It's sweet," he said. "I got used to bland flavors."

"When you were a prisoner?" she asked, taking another swallow and hoping the drink would relax her. As it was, she sounded like an interrogator.

Zayn twitched, but nodded. "The Kronock aren't much for appealing food. Most of what they eat is glorified mush."

Another big gulp and Katie felt her arms begin to tingle. She looked hard at the big muscular guy across from her and felt a tingle someplace much lower as well. She shifted in her chair, leaning forward and dropping her voice. "Was it awful?"

He met her gaze, and she saw something dark flash within it. "Let's say I'm glad not to be there anymore."

"Why do you think they took you?" she asked. "Were they trying to get command codes from you?"

He tilted his head at her. "Command codes? I am not a commander." He stared into his wine glass. "They knew they were not taking anyone important."

"Don't you think you're selling yourself short?" She tried to bat her eyelashes, but felt ridiculous and ended up looking away.

"Is something wrong with your eye?" he asked.

It took all her self-composure not to sigh. "Nope." She took a swig of wine. "So how were you able to escape?"

He shuddered as he thought back to working on his chains. "It took a long time, but I found some metal and filed at my shackles until they were weak enough to snap. Then I overpowered a guard and snuck off."

"And they didn't come after you?"

"No. I doubt they wanted to start a war by entering Drexian space after me."

"Don't they want a war anyway?" Katie asked. " From what everyone says, those scaly creeps aren't into diplomacy."

The edges of Zayn's mouth twitched. "Who told you they were scaly creeps?"

"Bridget. She's the only person I've met who's seen them." She hesitated. "Aside from you."

"Which one is Bridget?"

"The pretty one with black hair. You saw her when you burst into the bunker."

"I did not burst," he said. "I was worried about you, and may have been walking fast."

She felt a flush of pleasure that he'd been worried about her. It had been a long time since someone had cared about her for a reason that didn't have to do with what she could do for them. She decided not to push him for more information and instead set down her glass and lifted the silver dome off her plate. "I hope you enjoy steak. I had the chef prepare filet mignon with new potatoes. I had a feeling you were a meat and potatoes kind of guy. They assured me this is actual beef, but after the food I've eaten today, I'm not promising anything."

He lifted his own dome. "It looks wonderful." He picked up his fork and poked the filet. "What is steak?"

Katie thought for a moment. "It's a type of protein we eat on Earth. If I tell you where it comes from, you may not want to eat it."

He nodded, jabbing his fork into it and lifting it from his plate.

"No, no, no," Katie jumped up, waving her hands, and giggling. The wine made her feel much lighter and happier than usual, and for a moment, she lost track of what she was supposed to be doing. "Let me show you how to cut it."

She went to his side of the table and helped him lower his filet. She put his knife and fork in his hands and positioned them over his plate. "Hold the meat with your fork, and cut it with the knife."

He sawed at the filet and the knife scraped the bottom of the plate, making Katie flinch from the sound. She ducked under his arm and sat on his lap, placing her hands under his and guiding them. "You don't need to do it so hard, unless the meat is really tough, which this isn't."

She noticed, then, that his arms had gone stiff and his breathing had stopped. Was he having some sort of panic attack? She twisted around and saw that his eyes were molten, the bright blue almost obliterated by dark pupils that flashed with desire. His arms encased hers, but weren't touching her, and he kept them bowed wide as if he was afraid to come one inch closer to her.

"Sorry," she said, her voice coming out as a breathy whisper without even trying. "I didn't mean to get in your personal space."

He didn't make a move, and as she shifted her weight on his lap, she felt his hard cock bump up against her leg. Her own body tingled from the fizzy Palaxian wine, and Katie was aware of her muscles tensing in response to his arousal. It struck her that she was playing with fire by trying to seduce a creature that could easily bench-press her over his head. She'd already seen how fruitless it would be to struggle against him, and her skin heated as she remembered the feeling of being trapped under his body with his cock thick between her thighs.

Was she really ready to sleep with him to get her story? Would she go that far for an exposé that would make her career? Or was this not really about the story, and more about wanting to feel the breathless surrender she'd felt the night before?

There was something about this Drexian that she trusted, and it had been a long time since she'd trusted a man. Or anyone. She knew it was stupid to trust someone she barely knew, much less an alien who was horny as hell. Hadn't she learned anything growing up with a con man?

Her eyes dropped to his lips and her resolve wavered. It had been a long time since she'd let her guard down and actually had fun. What the hell, she thought as she lowered her lips to his. Unless these aliens had developed reanimation, you only lived once.

Chapter Nineteen

Zayn dropped the silverware and wrapped one arm around her waist, tangling the other in her hair and pulling her mouth in deeper to his. He loved the taste of her, and the feel of her tongue against his sent currents of pleasure through his body.

He knew he shouldn't be doing this. She was too good for him. He was disgraced warrior. He needed to focus on what was important. But what was that? He couldn't remember. He'd wanted to tell her something, hadn't he? All he knew was he hadn't felt this good in a long time, possibly ever, and he didn't want it to end.

She moaned in his mouth and pressed her body to his, the points of her nipples grazing his chest. He slid his hands down until he held her by the hips, swiveling her until she was straddling him and had wrapped her legs around his waist. Grinding against him, she intensified her kiss and raked her hands across his back, her fingers catching on his hard nodes.

Even though the Kronock had used the bumps along his spine to torture him, he had healed, and his nodes were even more sensitive than before. The feel of her fingertips made him convulse, the need coursing through him. He needed her. Needed to bury himself inside her so he could forget all the pain and loss.

She pulled back and held his gaze, breathing heavily as she rubbed his hot, engorged nodes with her thumbs. "Do you like this? Is this the way you do it?"

He arched into her hands as his answer, getting a jolt from each touch to his sensitive bumps.

She grinned and pulled at her bottom lip with her teeth, watching him. "Do you want more?"

He leveled his gaze at her. "I want everything."

Her green eyes widened slightly before she smiled again and lowered her head to his neck, biting him hard as she moved her hips. The nip made him growl and slide his hands down to cup her ass, moving the silk so his hands were underneath the fabric of her dress. He loved the softness of her, the curves that felt so good after living in a dank cell with nothing but hard, cold metal.

Zayn slipped one finger underneath the panties that were as soft as her dress and felt that she was damp. She bowed back as he stroked his finger between her legs, her moan throaty. He hadn't expected her to be completely bare—he'd thought human females had hair —but the skin beneath his finger was smooth and slick.

"Surprised?" she asked, her voice breathy as she leaned her head close to his. "I like to be smooth."

"You're my first human," he said. "Everything is a surprise."

She rolled her hips so that his finger slid inside, and she gasped. "I'm your only human."

His cock throbbed as he worked his finger deeper, feeling her tight folds clench around him. "And I am your only Drexian."

"Yeah, you are." Her words were breathy and vibrated against his ear. "Why don't you show me what Drexians can do?"

She crushed her mouth to his, and he tasted the sweet Palaxian wine on her tongue as it met his. He stroked his finger farther inside her, as he brought his other hand to the back of her head, pulling her deeper into the kiss. Desire pounded through him as both his tongue and finger caressed her, and he savored the intoxicating feel of her wet heat. The curious Katie who asked him questions and hung on his every word had vanished, and the seductress who'd replaced her drove him to the brink of sanity.

With a growl, Zayn stood, pushing the chair back so suddenly it clattered to the floor. Her legs were wrapped around his waist and she didn't stop kissing him as he strode to the bed, tearing aside the sheer fabric hanging around it. Lowering her onto her back, he leaned back and drank in the sight of her. Her skin was flushed pink, her red waves fanned out around her head, and the dress had slipped up to expose the sliver of black silk between her legs. He knew he didn't deserve something so perfect, but he couldn't deny her or himself.

He ran one hand up her stomach, bunching up her dress and revealing her panties. Slipping a finger through the string at one side, he ripped them off her in one motion. She yelped as he caught her by the ankles and pulled her so her legs straddled his hips.

"Do you want me to stop?" he asked, watching her nipples strain against the thin fabric of her dress.

She shook her head, her eyes burning as they locked with his, but the only noise she made was the sharp intake of breath as he drew his hands down the length of her thighs until his thumbs touched where she opened to him.

Where the black panties had been, there were only soft pink folds of her silken skin. Seeing her smooth bareness made a low rumble escape his throat. He dropped down and, taking her ass in both hands, he parted her with his thumbs. She was wet and ready, and he inhaled her feminine scent, his cock pulsing.

He trailed his tongue up, loving the taste of her, until he reached her swollen nub, then began licking. Her breath became jagged, and she gave a hoarse scream as he swirled his tongue over her, her hips twitching restlessly.

As she began to jerk, Zayn slipped a finger inside her, feeling her muscles tense as she bucked up and screamed. The sound of her pleasure enflamed him, but he kept sucking her slick nub as she trembled and her legs went slack. Need tore through Zayn as he reared back and jerked his pants down to let his cock spring free, fisting it in one hand and staring down at the woman so wet and ready for him.

Chapter Twenty

When Katie saw him pump his long, thick cock, her mouth went dry. It was one thing to feel it through his pants or even against her leg, but it was another to see it up close and personal. Her confidence faltered for a moment as her eyes moved from his cock to his stomach tight with strain to his sculpted chest muscles glistening with sweat. Even though he was big enough to crush her and powerful enough to tear her in two, she knew she didn't have to be afraid of this man. Instinctively she trusted him, even though everything about him raised more questions.

His piercing blue eyes locked with hers, and all thoughts of her plan had fled her mind. She didn't care about getting information from him, or learning about the Kronock, or even about breaking the alien abduction story. The only thing she could think about was how good Zayn made her feel and how much she wanted him.

But first, she wanted to return the favor. Sitting up, Katie grasped the base of his cock and heard him suck in a sharp breath as she leaned down.

"You don't have to," he said, his voice strangled.

She licked the tip, and a groan escaped him. "I want to."

Katie fisted him, pumping up and down as she took his crown into her mouth. His skin was like velvet, warm and soft despite his cock being as rigid and unyielding as granite. She swirled her tongue around him and looked up to see his head arched back, his ridged stomach taut. "Do you like this?"

He lowered his gaze to hers, his pupils flaring as watched her drag her tongue up his length. "There is not a way you could touch me I would not enjoy."

"Sweet talker." She smiled as she sucked his head into her mouth again.

Zayn brushed her curls off her face and took the back of her head in his hands, cradling her as she drew him in deeper. He moaned, his eyes half-lidded as she took his shaft deep into her throat.

Katie breathed out as she tried to take as much of his huge cock as she could. She'd definitely never had one this big, so she took him slow, sucking him in an inch at a time. She looked up as she swallowed him, loving the pleasure she saw on his face, even as he clearly fought for control, his lips pressed together. She sucked harder. When his crown reached the back of her throat, she constricted the muscles in her mouth, and his hands jerked in her hair.

"Grek," he whispered, his eyes scorching as he watched her.

She slid her mouth up and down his cock even as she gripped his base, going deeper with each stroke until his crown hit the back of her throat and she squeezed. He spasmed as his fingers tangled in her hair, and he pushed his hips forward to hold himself there.

"I've never felt . . ." he began before his words drifted off into an unintelligible groan.

She pulled back, drawing her lips slowly down his length until she reached the tip. "No one's ever done this to you?"

He stroked a finger down her cheek. "No one with lips as pretty as yours or a mouth as hot and tight."

She sank her mouth over his cock again, sliding up and down as she sucked. She loved the feel of him, and how her mouth had made his blue eyes almost black with desire. She moved faster, pumping him in a steady rhythm.

Zayn grunted and pulled away from her. "As much as I like watching that pretty mouth of your stretched around my cock, I want to see it split you even more."

He reached down and ripped her dress up and over her head with one hand, exposing her breasts and making a strangled noise in the back of his throat. He ran both hands down the length of her body as he pushed her back on the bed, his rough fingers feather-light as the tips caressed her.

She let her legs fall open, her body throbbing and aching for him to fill her. "I need you inside me, Zayn."

"Not yet." He pulled her up, flipping around so he sat on the edge of the bed with her straddling him. She whimpered as he bent and kissed each of her nipples, swirling his tongue around them. "So pink and perfect."

He sucked one into his mouth, making her arch into him, his hands firmly on her back and holding her in place. She dropped her hands and ran them through his hair as her legs tightened around his back. His mouth felt so good, but she wanted more, and she knew he was holding back. Was he afraid to hurt her?

She watched him teasing her nipples and reached around to his nodes, feeling his body tense as she rubbed first one, then another. They hardened under her touch until they were like granite. Moving her hips, his cock nestled between her folds. He moaned.

"So close," she whispered. "Don't you want that big cock inside me?"

He looked up at her. "You're too…"

"Too what?" She cut him off, not wanting to hear the reasons why. "Too wet? Too ready to take you deep?"

His eyes rolled back in his head as she ground against him. "Too perfect." The words came through gritted teeth. "I don't deserve to have you."

Her body burned with the desperate desire to have him inside her. She needed to feel claimed by this Drexian who wanted to protect her. She put her hands on the sides of his face and forced her to meet her gaze. "I am far from perfect, Zayn, and I think you do deserve me."

She'd just have to show him she wasn't as fragile as he thought. Using her feet to press down on the bed, Katie lifted herself so that his thick crown was notched at her slick opening. His eyes widened as she lowered herself onto him. The air left her as she took him all the way.

"I'm too big," he said, the strain in his voice clear.

She raised herself and came down on him again, stretching around him and loving the sensation of his cock lodged deep. "No. I like it." She let out a whispery moan. "I like being filled by you."

He held her as she moved her hips. "You're so tight. I don't want to hurt you."

She took his face in hers. "You won't break me, Zayn." She kissed him, nipping his bottom lip. "I promise."

"So tight," he murmured, his voice a husky purr. "Tight and perfect."

"I'm not perfect, but I am yours."

He thrust up into her. "Mine." The word sounded hesitant at first, but he slammed his hips up once more, his voice louder. "All mine."

Her nails scraped his back as she cried out. "Yes!"

He thrust up again, and she met his stroke with one of her own. The feel of him ignited her, making her mind a swirl of desire and need and leaving all rational thought behind. There was nothing but Zayn right there in that moment, his body locked with hers.

They found a rhythm, her breaths turning to pants as they moved together and her breasts bounced with each hard thrust. Katie spread her legs wider, moving her legs back and tilting her hips so her clit rubbed against him with each stroke. Her legs trembled as her release grew, first a low simmer she felt in her belly, building to an explosion that tore through her as her body clamped onto his cock.

"That's right," he said, his voice hoarse. "I want to feel you squeezing me."

His words made her scream as more surges of pleasure coursed through her.

Zayn kept himself buried in her as he stood and spun her onto her back, his weight pressing her into the bed. She loved how big he felt covering her body with his own.

He powered into her, drilling his cock deeper than before. Katie opened her mouth to scream but his deep thrusts knocked the wind out of her. She gasped as he pounded into her again and again, holding her legs over his shoulders. She knew she shouldn't want to surrender to him like this, but she did. She loved the feeling of being taken by him, his big body claiming her smaller one, his bronze skin dark against hers, and his callused hands grasping her hips desperately as he chased his release.

"Come inside me," she said, her words escaping between gasps. "I want to feel it."

Her words seemed to push him over the edge. He roared and gave a final push, his hot pulses filling her. Zayn collapsed, bracing himself with his elbows so he wouldn't crush her, but his body pressed flush against hers.

Katie felt his heart hammering as if it was her own, and she pulled him closer.

Chapter Twenty-One

Zayn woke when it was still dark. He rolled over in bed, his legs tangling in the sheet as he reached for Katie. They'd barely crawled up to the pillows and collapsed after slaking their thirst for each other twice more. Even now, he felt boneless. His pulse quickened as he thought back to watching her as she took all of him—her eyes flaring, her cheeks flushed, and her curls wild. The memory of her wet heat, so tight as he'd pushed inside her, made him almost moan out loud.

His hands groped for her soft form beneath the sheets, but her side of the bed was empty. He pushed himself up, scanning the room. The nearly full moon sent light spilling across the balcony, but he could see she was not out there, or in the sitting area to the other side of the bed. He forced down a rising sense of panic as he stood, not bothering to dress as he took long steps toward the door.

As he drew even with the bathroom door, he paused. Soft light came from inside, along with humming. The high-pitched humming of a song.

He pushed the door open all the way and his shoulders relaxed as he saw Katie stretched out in the standing tub. Her head lolled

129

back on one end, while her crossed feet poked out of the other, bubbles billowing up in the middle. A few electronic glowing pillar candles sat on the marble countertop, illuminating the room. He didn't know if the sweet scent came from the candles or the bath, but it filled the room and made him think of flowers.

She hummed as she moved her feet back and forth, following an invisible beat only she knew. He watched her as he stood in the doorway, memorizing the sight of her fiery curls piled on top of her head, a few wet tendrils curling around her neck. The flickering candlelight made her skin look golden as it danced across her slender neck and the arms she draped along the edges of the tub. Everything about her was so feminine and delicate it made his heart clench with an overpowering need to protect her. Even from himself.

As if sensing his presence, she turned her head and smiled. "Did I wake you?"

He shook his head and walked closer, aware that he was naked and the sight of her was sending blood south. "Could you not sleep?"

Her smile flickered. "I woke up and couldn't fall back asleep, so I thought I'd come in here and take advantage of this amazing tub." She scooped up a handful of bubbles. "Did you know there's a button you press for bubbles, and another for bath oil, and another for bath salts?"

He laughed, her wonder at the high-tech bathroom contagious. "You like it?"

She sank down a fraction, the bubbles covering her neck. "I may never leave."

"I would be fine with that." He leaned against the counter and watched her. "As long as you didn't mind company every so often."

Katie wiggled her brows. "Care to join me now?"

He eyed the bubbles cresting the rim. "Are you sure I'll fit and not make you lose all your water?"

"You worry a lot about things fitting," she said, giving him a wicked smile. "Didn't I tell you I could take you?"

Zayn couldn't help chuckling. "Don't say you didn't ask for it."

"Never," she said with mock seriousness as he stepped into the tub and lowered himself so he faced her, water and bubbles sloshing over the side and onto the floor.

She waved a hand. "We've got towels to soak it all up later."

She shimmied as he stretched his long legs on either side of her, bowing them so he surrounded her body and his feet hooked behind her ass. Katie bent her legs over his thighs and rested her arms on his knees as they poked above the water's surface. "You make a pretty good lounge chair."

His muscles relaxed as he breathed in the fragrant steam and slid down to let the warm water cover his chest. "This does feel nice."

"What did I tell you?" She traced a finger lazily on his knee. "Enough warm water can make you forget all your worries."

He closed his eyes and let his head rest against the smooth surface of the tub. As good as it felt, he couldn't imagine ever forgetting the images that haunted his sleep, or the worries that filled his waking hours. He wished he could forget it all. He wished none of it had ever happened and he didn't feel so damaged. The only time he'd felt whole again was when he'd been inside her, when it felt like she'd been the missing part of him the Kronock had taken.

"You want to tell me?" Katie asked.

He opened his eyes to see her watching him. "Tell you?"

"Why your face is twisted up like you're being tortured." Her words caught in her throat. "I'm sorry. That wasn't what you were thinking about, was it? Being tortured?"

He took her hand. "No, not really. I was thinking about you."

She tilted her head at him. "If thinking of me makes you scrunch up your face like that, I'm not sure if that's a good thing."

"I don't want to hurt you."

She squeezed his hand. "You won't. I know you won't."

"My nightmares," he said. "You've seen what they're like. What if I…?"

She sat up. "I may not have known you long, but I *know* you. I've seen how you worry about me, how you want to protect me, how you look at me. You won't hurt me."

As she looked at him, her eyes earnest, he had to tell her. "The pains in my head, the ones that happen every time the station malfunctions?" He took a breath. "It's not normal. I don't feel normal."

"Of course you don't. You've been through something awful. It would be odd if you did feel normal."

He dropped his eyes. "What if they did something to me? The Kronock? What if the pains aren't just residual effects from torture? What if they're more?"

"Didn't the doctors check you out when you escaped?" she asked, rubbing her thumb over the back of his hand.

"Yes, but the High Command expedited my rehab. They said I'd been through enough."

"I can see their point, but you'd think they'd want to make sure you're okay before giving you the 'all-clear,'" Katie said. "Why don't you go back to the medical bay? Mandy works there sometimes. She's another tribute bride, and Dorn's wife. I'm sure she'd listen to you and take you seriously."

He hated the thought of the sterile medical bay. Even though it was well lit and pristine, the metal tools and shiny devices gave him flashbacks of being on the Kronock torture table.

"Brown hair?" he asked. "Straight and long?"

"Mandy?" Katie said. "Yeah, she was also here the first time we met, although I was less thrilled with her then."

"I also remember her from when I arrived at the station and they were treating my wounds. She was nice to me."

"See?" She dribbled some of the bubbly water onto his leg. "I'll go with you, if you'd like. Mandy owes me one, anyway. More than one, actually."

He nodded, looking at her, his chest constricting. He knew without a doubt he didn't deserve her, but he didn't care. She was his.

"So stop worrying so much." She splashed him gently. "Unless you're worried about hurting me with that huge cock, in which case, I'm fine with that."

He felt his cock twitch.

"I like that kind of hurt," she said, grinning at him. "You want me to show you how much I like it?"

He couldn't answer as she slid her body toward his, but he dropped his hands into the water and grabbed her ass, lifting her so he held one round cheek in each hand.

The water made everything slippery. He felt her hand as she reached down and dragged his cockhead through her folds. She arched her back as she rubbed him over her clit, back and forth until her breath was jagged. Her full breasts bobbed in the water, and Zayn took one in each hand, thumbing her nipples as she stroked herself with his cock.

She moved faster, her hips moving as she worked herself on him. Her closed eyelids fluttered as her head bent back.

"Look at me, cinnara," he said. "I want your eyes on me when you come."

She jerked up and met his eyes, hers hot with desire. A few more moves, and she shattered with a scream, her body bucking but her eyes never leaving his.

Zayn waited for her to sag into him before lifting her and turning her so her body spooned his, her legs stretching alongside his. Her head fell back onto his chest as she regained her breath.

"I'm not done with you yet," he said, grasping her hips and moving her up so his cock notched between her ass cheeks.

She spread her legs while still stretched out on top of his body, letting him slip the broad crown of his cock inside her, holding her breath while he slowly dragged her down until she'd taken him to the hilt.

"Is this the kind of hurt you like?" he whispered in her ear.

Her response was a throaty sigh. "Mmm-hmm."

He rotated her hips so she was sitting up and began lifting her up and down on his cock, feeling her heat mix with the warmth of the water. She moaned every time their bodies met; flesh hitting flesh and water splashing around them. She raised her hands to cup her own breasts.

"Harder, Zayn. I want it harder."

As he felt the liquid heat coil in his belly, he sat up on his knees and bent her over so her hands clutched the edge of the tub. Their bodies were mostly out of the water, and he watched as his cock entered her from behind. He pulled out until he saw his slick, swollen crown, then he slowly pushed it inside her, savoring the sight of her stretching to take him. He stroked in again, this time thrusting hard. Katie screamed.

He paused, but she shook her head, swiveling around to meet his eyes. "Don't stop. Don't ever stop."

He buried himself again as she gasped, her knuckles white against the edge of the tub. All he could think about when his cock was lodged inside her was her. Katie belonged to him. Her moans and screams were for him. Only him.

Reaching around, Zayn found her nub and swirled his finger as he thrust his cock deep. Her hips jerked, but he held her steady as she rippled around him, her muscles pulsing. She screamed his name as she came, and he felt the blood rushing in his head as his own need pounded through him. Digging his fingers into her soft hips, he hammered into her as he climaxed, feeling nothing but the sensations of her wet heat quivering around him and wave after wave of contentment crashing over him.

Chapter Twenty-Two

Katie ran her hands through her hair and felt the curls still damp at the nape of her neck. She'd crept out of bed and dressed in black yoga pants and a pink T-shirt, moving quietly so as not to wake Zayn as he slept soundly, his long limbs sprawled across the bed.

Tiptoeing to the balcony, she spotted the sun cresting the trees in the distance. Slats of warm light bathed the grassy savannah and reached the wood railing. A group of zebra grazed only feet away, so Katie lowered herself into a lounge chair as silently as possible. A bird squawked as it flew low, but the zebras ignored it.

It amazed her that the artificial environment smelled like morning, with the fresh scent of dew hanging in the air. A fine mist even covered the arms of her chair. She wiped it away, thinking what an impressive job the Drexians had done creating holographic worlds that even felt and smelled right. They'd even improved upon it, since they hadn't recreated bugs. She didn't have to worry about being nipped at by gnats or feasted on by mosquitos.

With a final look back at Zayn, Katie took out a notepad and pen she'd found in the nightstand. Despite how amazing last night had been, she wasn't ready to give up her chance to get back to Earth. Staying with a hot alien had seemed like a good idea when she was rolling around in bed with him, but that wasn't real life. Her practical side wouldn't let her believe in her feelings over what made sense. And getting back to Earth made logical sense. No matter what her heart told her.

She tapped the pen on the paper and tried to think back to the night before and what Zayn had told her. Memories flooded her mind, but not of their conversation. Her face warmed as she thought of their bodies locked together, of the water splashing out of the tub, and of their mingled screams of pleasure. She glanced at the empty paper. She was definitely not writing any of that down.

She needed to take notes about what she'd learned so far, since she didn't trust herself to remember all of it later. There was too much. Details, she thought. She should start with details. She thought of all the incredible things about the space station and alien technology.

No bugs, she wrote. *Levitating bar stools. Floating food carts. Bathtubs with instant bubbles.*

She crossed out what she'd written and frowned. All those things were cool but they didn't strike her as things that would make her story believable.

Implants to translate alien languages, she wrote. Now that was something that couldn't be explained away. *Ships that travel at the speed of light. Can fly to Saturn in under two hours.*

She bit the end of her pen. *Nodes.*

She twisted around to look at Zayn again, her heart thumping as she thought about his nodes hardening under her touch. She let out a breath as she saw he was still sleeping. Her stomach tightened as her focus returned to her notes.

What was she going to do about Zayn? Getting off the station and getting back to Earth so she could write her story meant that she'd never see him again. It wasn't like she could take him with her, even if he agreed to come, which she knew he wouldn't and couldn't do.

A Drexian warrior as big as him would not blend in on Earth. Even if he convinced people he was a bodybuilder, what would he do down there? There wasn't much call for galactic warriors in LA. At least, not real ones. And he would never abandon his people, especially not if there was the threat of invasion. Katie would never ask him to do that, which left her right back where she started. Escaping the station meant leaving him forever.

She swallowed hard. What was the big deal? She'd only known him for a few days. Besides, leaving people was her specialty. She didn't get attached. You had to trust to get attached, and her father had taught her never to trust anyone.

So why did she trust a big alien she'd just met? Maybe because he was the first person in a long time, maybe ever, who'd worried about her more than himself. Knowing that Zayn wanted to protect her made her trust him. She knew in her gut he would never hurt her or leave her or do any of the other things people in her past had done that had made her doubt herself.

"Get it together, Katie," she whispered to herself, hearing her father's voice echo in her head.

Even if she did trust him, care about him, even, that didn't mean she could change all her plans. One thing she'd learned long ago was not to rearrange her life around a man. And abandoning her story and her plan to escape from the space station would mean that she was changing everything for him. She pressed her lips together. Some part of herself deep inside couldn't let her do that, even though her heart ached at the thought of leaving.

Katie began writing an introduction to her article, the lines flowing as she wrote. After about half a page, she paused and reread what she'd written. Not a bad start, but she needed more about the Kronock. She didn't know much about them yet. She'd have to try to learn more about where they came from, and how the war between the Kronock and the Drexians started. Zayn would be able to tell her.

She'd tried to push the thought of Zayn from her mind and take him out of the equation, but he kept creeping back in. He would be crushed if she left. She knew from the way he looked at her and the way he touched her that he was already in deep. Her pulse fluttered. Hell, maybe she was, too.

What was the alternative? Stay with him? Marry him? Live her life with an alien on a space station no one on Earth knew about and never set foot on her home planet again? She allowed herself to imagine life with Zayn and couldn't help smiling.

The sun had risen above the trees, and the golden rays warmed her bare feet. She let her head lean back as she breathed in the faint scent of gardenia. It sure beat the one-bedroom in the Valley she'd been living in, the one she couldn't even afford. And she knew she'd never find a man in LA, maybe in all of California, who would look at her the way he did. Not to mention the way he made her feel.

She huffed out her breath, impatient with herself. She needed to focus. If she couldn't concentrate on writing, she could brainstorm places she wanted to pitch her story when she returned to Earth. At the bottom of the page, she made a to-do list of things to do upon her return under the heading "Back on Earth" along with the top publications and tabloid TV shows she knew would want her exposé. As much as the publication made her cringe, she felt sure *The National Enquirer* would pay top dollar.

Zayn rolled over in bed, making a small grunting sound. Katie turned to see the sheet slip off and expose his perfect ass. Nope. She was sure she'd never land one of those back on Earth.

As she watched him sleep she thought back to the first night they'd been in bed, of his nightmares, of the torture he'd withstood, of the pains in his head. Then she thought of him telling her his worries about the pains. He'd trusted her.

Katie looked at her "Back on Earth" checklist and shame washed over her. She ripped the page off the notepad and folded it in half. She couldn't do it. She couldn't leave him. Not yet, at least. Not when he was so vulnerable.

Katie padded across the suite and slipped the folded paper, notepad, and pen into the nightstand drawer on her side, sliding them to the back. Zayn groaned and opened one eye, looking at her and closing it again.

"Why are you awake?" he asked.

"It's morning. I was enjoying the sunrise on the balcony." She sat on the edge of the bed and touched his stubbly cheek. "Did you know the sun rises and sets in the same place here?"

"Really?" He didn't sound impressed by this.

"Think about it, if they designed it like a regular sunrise and sunset, we'd miss one of them because our balcony faces one direction. But you Drexians are so clever." She ran a hand through his hair. "Since it's a hologram, you make it so that we get perfect sunrises and perfect sunsets."

"I guess that's why they're called fantasy suites," Zayn mumbled.

Katie giggled. "Am I just finding out that you're not a morning person?"

"It's not that I'm *not* a morning person," Zayn said, as he rolled onto his back, taking the sheet with him, and opened his eyes. "But I don't remember us sleeping much during the night."

"That's a fair point." She leaned down and kissed him, her lips lingering on his.

"Now I remember why I didn't get any sleep," he said, pulling her back. "And why I didn't care."

Katie saw the bulge under the sheet growing. She leaned into his kiss, feeling his need, and moaning as his tongue parted her lips. She sat up and stepped out of his reach. "Sorry, buddy. You snooze, you lose."

He furrowed his brow. "I do not understand this game."

She tapped her wrist even though she wore no watch. "I ordered breakfast, which should be here soon."

"How soon?" Zayn glanced down at the tented sheet.

She crossed her arms. "Probably before Serge and Reina get here."

That made him sit up. "They're coming here? Now?" He slid out of bed, not bothering to cover himself as he scooped up his boxer briefs and drawstring pants from the floor and tugged them on.

"I think you have time to put on clean clothes," she said, walking to the dresser and opening a drawer at the bottom. "Look. More pants." She pawed through the pile. "I bet you'd look good in these cargo pants."

"Better than I look in these?" he asked.

She twisted around to appraise the soft pants that left little to imagination, and her eyes lingered on the huge bulge that had not deflated. "Maybe not, but you should probably wear them anyway."

Katie tossed the black cargo pants to him along with a fresh pair of dark-gray boxer briefs. She watched him change, even though a part of her felt she should look away. She almost laughed, considering how much of each other they'd seen the night before.

She swallowed hard as he stood before her shirtless with the cargo pants dipping below his waist. "I should be back soon. I think today I'm picking out flowers, or maybe it's music. I forget."

He crossed to her and wrapped his arms around her waist. "I will be here when you return."

Her body warmed in response to his touch and the brush of his lips across hers. "I'm counting on it."

A rap on the door made her sigh.

"I'll get it." He reached the door in a few long strides, holding it open for the Gatazoid who bustled in with the floating food cart.

Katie could smell the blend of savory and sweet smells even before he lifted the silver domes from the plates. Her nose twitched at one particular scent. "Do I smell coffee?"

The small alien nodded. "I was told you required the stimulant."

"You were told right," Katie murmured, gratefully taking the cup he offered her and inhaling the aroma with her eyes closed.

"I believe I am jealous," Zayn said, as he watched her.

She smiled at him as she took a sip. "You should be. This tastes almost like a Starbucks mocha."

His eyes went to the plates and his own lips curled into a smile. "More sugary rings."

Katie picked up a doughnut and held it out to him to bite. "I figured this was why you tasted so sweet when you kissed me yesterday."

He cocked an eyebrow at her. "When *I* kissed *you*?"

"Or when I kissed you," she said, her cheeks flushing. "Whatever."

He swallowed the bite of doughnut and swept her up into a kiss, his tongue tangling with hers before he released her. "Like that?"

She felt dazed as she touched a finger to her lips. "Just like that."

"Looks like we're right on time," Serge said, as he clomped into the room, a thick binder tucked under his arm.

Katie snatched up a doughnut and took a bite. Knowing Serge, they'd be so busy with wedding planning she wouldn't get another bite to eat. "Want one?" she asked Reina, who'd walked in behind Serge.

"We don't have your tolerance for sweet things," Serge said, before Reina could answer, wrinkling his nose at the sticky doughnut.

"Speak for yourself," Zayn said, pulling Katie into another long kiss.

Chapter Twenty-Three

Zayn finish the sugary ring, licking his fingers after he was done. He took a sip of the moi moi juice, after taking a swallow of the coffee that Katie loved so much and cringing. He thought humans loved sugar. The black, hot drink was bitter and tasted burnt, with no hint of sweetness. He took another bite of the sugar ring his mate had called a doughnut. Now these, he could get used to, especially if she liked kissing him after he'd eaten them.

Thinking of Katie and her soft kisses made his heart beat faster. He still felt like he was basking in the night before, his muscles loose and the worry that usually plagued him seemingly driven from his mind. Being with her was like nothing else he'd experienced before. He'd never been much for the females on the pleasure planets. Encounters with them were empty and hollow. Katie was different. He loved that she looked soft, yet had an inner fire and determination. Not to mention the side of her he'd seen when she'd straddled him and taken charge.

Thinking about her fiery side made his cock strain against his pants, which was painful, since the cargo pants were not as forgiving as the drawstring ones. He readjusted himself and put down the moi moi juice. That would have to wait until later, as would his thoughts of his mate. He did not want her to come back finding him stroking himself in the shower because he couldn't stop thinking about her and how perfect she'd looked riding his cock.

Since she was off doing wedding things, Zayn had time to go to the medical bay. He reflexively raised a hand to his head. It hadn't hurt since the day before, but the station also hadn't experienced any malfunction. More than ever, Zayn was convinced the two were connected. He didn't know how, but he had to find out.

Talking with Katie about the pains in his head had made him realize that he needed to figure out what was going on. Sharing his fears with her had made him feel better, as had her confidence in him. He knew from the look in her eyes that she didn't believe he could do anything bad, and looking at her almost made him believe it, too. She'd offered to go with him, but knowing Serge, she'd be busy most of the day. As much as he liked having her close to him, he didn't need her by his side to do this. He might be damaged, but he was still a Drexian warrior.

No, he would go to the medical bay without her and see if Mandy was there. For whatever reason he felt more comfortable around a human than he did sharing his pains with a fellow Drexian. Warriors were trained to hide their pain, not complain about it. Although Zayn was not complaining, he worried it might appear that way.

He pulled on a shirt and tucked it half into the black cargo pants. He found a familiar yet new pair of military-grade boots and slipped his feet into them, welcoming the weight and feel as he strode out of the suite and toward that inclinator. Even though he was going to do something he dreaded, he couldn't help smiling as he stepped into the sleek compartment and swiped a hand across the panel. He could still smell Katie on him, and the sweet scent of the bath. He sniffed his arm and almost laughed as he wondered if others could smell the floral scent on him, as well. So much for his reputation as a tough guy. Even the scars wouldn't help if he smelled like a flower.

It didn't take him long to go the few floors down to the medical bay. He flinched at the antiseptic smell as the double doors swished open, the scent bringing him back to the time he'd spent there while his broken ribs had healed, and tests had been run. Now, he was glad the perfume of his skin could combat the chemical smell.

Zayn scanned the wide room, taking in the levitating beds and metal arms that swung down from the ceiling. Scanners beeped, and there was a low hum of hushed conversations. A few medics in white uniforms directed hovering carts of surgical tools beside them as they crossed the room. His eyes searched the staff until he spotted the human with long brown hair.

He didn't know much about Mandy, except that she was mated with Dorn, the commander of the Inferno Force. That, and she was somehow the reason Katie was on the boat and matched with him in the first place. Even though he hadn't understood all the details, he gathered that Mandy and Katie's paths had crossed on Earth, somehow. Mandy's disappearance had resulted in Katie getting in trouble, so the Drexians had solved Katie's problem by bringing her to the Boat. At Mandy's insistence.

He remembered Katie had not been pleased when she first met Mandy and made the connection, but from what she told him last night, Katie had decided to move on and make friends with Mandy. He didn't know if it was forgiveness or practicality, since Mandy was one of a limited number of human women on the station. Either way, she'd sent him to confide in Mandy, so Katie must trust the woman.

As he stood in the doorway not knowing quite what to do, Mandy saw him and waved.

"Zayn! What are you doing here?" She walked quickly across the room, holding an electronic tablet with one hand.

"Katie suggested I come see you," he said.

Her eyebrows rose. "Really? About what?"

He cleared his throat and glanced around, his confidence waning as he noticed the Drexians giving him curious looks. Mandy seemed to pick up on his discomfort.

She took him by one arm and walked him to the hovering bed at the far end of the room. "Here, this is better. Now we can talk without all those busybodies listening."

He managed a smile as he sat on the wide of the hoverbed. He wasn't sure what a "busybody" was, but the way she spoke reminded him of Katie, and he felt some of the tension leave his body.

"Please remove your clothing," a robotic voice said, making Zayn jump and swivel his head around.

Mandy sighed. "I spoke too soon." She tilted her head up and raised her voice. "Thanks, Al, but we don't need you to examine him yet. I'm giving him a quick scan."

"Who are you talking to?" Zayn asked, seeing nobody nearby who looked like an "Al."

Mandy smiled. "Al is the nickname Bridget gave this artificial intelligence medical program she met when she was taken by the Kronock." She fluttered a hand at him. "It's a long story, but when they blew up the enemy outpost, the Drexian team saved Al and brought him here. He's actually pretty helpful, even if he's a bit bossy."

"I am not bossy," Al said, his words halting. "I am efficient."

Zayn shivered, the mechanical voice reminding him of the partly-robotic Kronock who'd held him captive. "Is it okay if we skip the AI examination this time?"

"You hear that, Al?" Mandy asked. "You can power down for now."

"As you wish, although I might remind you that I am programmed with the medical knowledge of hundreds of species?"

Mandy rolled her eyes. "Yeah, you've mentioned that before." She turned back to Zayn. "Now it's really just us, so what's the problem?"

"It's probably nothing, but I've been having shooting pains in my head ever since I got back."

"You mean, since you escaped from the Kronock" Even though she said it matter-of-factly, he couldn't help flinching. He guessed his imprisonment and torture weren't a secret, especially in the medical bay, and especially for Dorn's wife.

He nodded. "I wouldn't think anything of it, if the pains didn't coincide with the malfunctions that have happened on the ship."

She looked up from where her finger had been tapping on the tablet. "So every time there's a malfunction your head hurts?"

"Well, not exactly." He glanced down at his feet. "My head begins to hurt before the malfunction. It's almost like my body can predict when they're going to happen."

She bit the edge of her lip. "I don't think that's entirely unusual. There are people on Earth who can predict the weather with a bum knee. At least, they say they can."

"You don't think I should be worried?"

Mandy looked over her shoulder. "Well, I'm not a doctor. To be honest, I'm not even a fully-trained medic. Why don't I do a scan and see if I can find anything."

He hesitated, glancing at the metal arms in the ceiling.

"Not the AI, I promise. I'll just use a handheld scanner. If I find anything, we can see what the doctor recommends we do next." She shrugged. "Chances are it's nothing and no one but us will ever need to know."

Zayn exhaled and gave her a weak smile. "Thanks. Katie said you'd know what to do."

Mandy shook her head, but he could tell she was pleased, her cheeks turning pink. "Like I said, I'm new to this, but I really love it. The medical advances you guys have made are incredible. I wish people on Earth could see all of this."

She directed him to lie back on the bed while she picked up a shiny, metal device from a nearby counter. "I always thought the things they had on *Star Trek* to diagnose and heal people were so cool, and then I come up here and find out that you guys have them. Or at least something like them."

Zayn focused on breathing in and out, closing his eyes so he wouldn't have to see the animatronic arms above him that were used for surgeries. Even the beep of the machines throughout the room made him think of the sounds of the mechanically enhanced Kronock, their red eyes flashing and their circuitry whirring. He knew not all of them were augmented, but the ones who'd tortured him had been. He always wondered if they used virtual robots so there would be no chance for compassion.

"I promise you won't feel a thing," Mandy said, then giggled. "Famous last words, right?"

He didn't understand Earth humor, but he opened his eyes and tried to laugh along with her. Mandy extended the device and pressed a button as she slowly moved it from his head all the way down to his feet and then back up again. She tapped her tablet and squinted. "That's odd."

Zayn sat up. "What's odd?" His stomach tightened as she pressed her brows together.

"I know you were examined when you got here, right?"

"Of course. I had a full workup. They said I was fine, aside for some breaks and bruises which they fixed." He glanced down at the scars on his arm. "And of course, the scars."

"I'm guessing Al didn't scan you, since you seemed surprised when he started talking."

"No Al," Zayn said. "Why?"

"That's what I thought. He never would have missed something like this." Mandy gnawed the edge of her lip again. "I'm still surprised a doctor missed it. Unless I'm reading this all wrong."

Zayn grabbed her arm and the woman looked up at him, her eyes wide. "Mandy, what is it?"

"There's something in your head." She dropped her voice to whisper. "It looks like there's something attached to your spine at the base of your brainstem."

Zayn touched a hand to the back of his neck, feeling a wave of nausea threaten to bring up every sugary bite of his breakfast. What had the Kronock done to him?

Chapter Twenty-Four

"What flavor did you say this was again?" Katie asked, as she took another tentative bite of a spongy, lime-colored cake, topped with a thick layer of ivory icing.

"Watermelon with a coconut-cream-cheese frosting," Reina said, reading from a tented sign on the table.

Katie swallowed and tried to smile. "I've never had watermelon cake before."

A round woman with dark skin, a pale-pink bob and oversized, owl-like glasses sat across from her, smiling and nodding. "I know. Isn't it fun? Why should wedding cakes be boring, that's what I say? Why not be adventurous? Mix things up?" She pushed a plate forward. "Try the sweet corn and banana."

Reina picked up a small, sample-sized plate with a sliver of neon-yellow cake with a black-dotted icing. "You're so creative, Sid. Who would have imagined?"

No one with any common sense, Katie thought. She put down the watermelon cake and took a sip of water to get the odd flavor combination out of her mouth. Instead of picking flowers for her wedding, Serge and Reina had led her to the station's only wedding cake baker.

The bakery wasn't a typical shop, in that it didn't sell pastries or cakes out of glass cases. It also didn't smell like a regular bakery, with sugar or yeast hanging thick in the air. The cacophony of scents in this kitchen made Katie's nose twitch.

Located behind the pretty promenade shops, the wedding cake bakery had a nondescript door with no awning, and looked more like a commercial kitchen inside. Stainless steel ovens ringed the walls, interspersed with flat surface burners. A mixer large enough for a toddler to stand in was tucked in the corner, and a giant refrigerator with glass doors sat across from them. Several high, metal tables occupied the center of the space. Katie and Reina sat on a pair of hovering barstools, while Sid perched on one across from them. Serge had left them, proclaiming that he never ate cake, and needed to check in with the dress designers.

Lucky bastard, Katie thought, as she eyed the rows of small, square plates lined up down the table.

"You don't happen to have any boring flavors, do you?" Katie asked.

Sid blinked a few times, her eyes enormous behind the round, black-rimmed glasses. "Would you consider sweet potato and salted caramel boring?"

"Not really."

The woman's name was Sid, which was short for an alien name so long and convoluted that Katie had merely gaped at her when she'd pronounced it. Sid was a Gatazoid, like Serge, but that was where the similarities ended. While the pint-sized wedding planner was wiry, Sid was as wide as she was tall. She wore a white chef's jacket that belled out around her legs like a tent, and clogs that didn't give her more than a couple of inches and looked more like Dutch wooden shoes than kitchen clogs. She did sound like Serge when she walked; heavy clomping accompanying her movements, but her voice was fast and chirpy, reminding Katie of a bird.

"No vanilla or chocolate?" Katie picked up one dark-red cake, hoping it might be red velvet, and tried not to groan when she read the tented card behind it that proclaimed it beet.

"Don't tell me you're one of those humans who likes typical cake flavors?" Sid fluttered a chubby hand in the air. "We do have to design flavors that all the guests will like, you know. Drexians aren't used to the sweet flavors you Earthlings prefer. They like bold, savory flavors that are more salty and Earthy."

That explained the cedar bark cake with black cherry icing.

"Does your groom like padwump?"

Katie remembered padwump from the breakfast tray, but could have sworn it was a crispy meat. "Isn't that like bacon?"

Sid grinned, her eyes huge and twinkling behind her enormous lenses. "I've been told humans love bacon. Put it everything."

Katie supposed that was true, but she still didn't want a bacon wedding cake. Or a padwump one.

"Zayn loves doughnuts," Katie said.

The baker flicked a hand through her cotton-candy-hued hair. "Does he now? That's intriguing." She slid off her stool and her clogs clomped to the floor. "I wonder if I could make a cake that tastes like a doughnut."

Katie was about to stop the woman and explain that she hadn't meant for her to bake a doughnut wedding cake, but then she stopped herself. Doughnut flavor was better than the cranberry-oregano concoction sitting in from of her.

"Just regular doughnut flavor, right?" Katie asked. "Not doughnut and dill pickle?"

Sid's laugh was a high, fast twitter. "Of course not." She stopped laughing. "Although I've never baked with pickle before."

Katie waved her hands. "Nope. No pickle. Zayn hates pickles."

Sid's face fell. "Too bad. I think you were on to something, dearie."

"Now that we have a flavor," Reina said through a mouthful of cake. "What would you like it to look like?"

Sid clip-clopped over to a steel shelving unit and pulled down what looked like a black cookie sheet. She set it down between Reina and Katie and swept a finger across the top. The surface immediately illuminated with an image of a cake that appeared to be hanging upside down.

"That's interesting," Katie said.

Sid shrugged. "It was until I discovered they were doing them on Earth." She swept her finger to the left and another image appeared, this one of a rainbow-colored cake where the colors appeared to be moving across the surface in a continual swirl.

Reina clapped her long hands. "That was one of my bride's. She said it reminded her of rainbows in Ireland. Apparently, they have lots of rain there and lots of rainbows."

Katie thought it looked more like an edible hallucination, but she decided not to point that out. "There's a tribute bride from Ireland here?" she asked instead.

Reina looked taken aback. "Of course. We have tributes from almost every country on your planet."

"I didn't know," Katie said, feeling instantly foolish. "I've only met women from the US so far."

Sid flipped to the next image. A completely round ball of orange cake seemed to hang in mid air.

"How do you cut a round cake?" Katie asked, tilting her head as she looked at the revolving cake.

"Very carefully," the baker said without a hint of humor in her voice.

"What about stacked cakes," Katie asked. "You know, one layer on top of the other getting smaller as they go up?"

Sid tapped her dimpled chin and flipped to a photo of a purple pyramid with a beam of light shooting out of the top.

Katie nodded. "Was that for a bride from Egypt?"

"No." Sid looked confused. "She was from a town called Las Vegas."

"Ah," Katie said as she noticed that the pyramid cake shimmered. "Now I get it." She sighed as the baker flipped through more images, each one crazier than the one before. "You don't have anything really boring, do you?"

Sid looked over her lenses. "You mean the Heartland Collection?"

Katie looked to Reina. "Do I?"

"Show her," Reina said, with a solemn bob of the head.

Sid pulled the screen back and her fingers danced across the screen before she set it back in front of them. The image was of a plain, ivory cake with six round tiers. The icing designs looked remarkably like the *Star Trek* insignia, but aside from that, it was simple and elegant and boring.

Katie slapped the metal table. "Yes! Like that, but without the icing symbols."

Sid let out a huff of breath. "I suppose you want it colorless, as well?"

"You mean white icing?" Katie asked. "That depends, what flavor is your white icing?"

She did not want her doughnut-flavored cake to be topped with tartar sauce buttercream.

Before Sid could answer, the doors behind them flew open.

"There you are," Mandy said rushing past Serge as he held the door open. "I've been looking everywhere for you."

"Luckily she ran into me while I was leaving the bridal salon," Serge said, smoothing his suit as he calmly walked toward them.

"Mandy?" Katie slid off her stool, surprised to see the woman looking so red-faced and disheveled. It looked like she'd run a mile in her clothes.

"We're picking cakes," Reina said, her usually sunny smile slipping as she took in Mandy's appearance. "Is everything okay?"

Mandy's eyes flicked to the Gatazoid baker. "Hi, Sid." She walked over to Katie and pulled her away by the sleeve, dropping her voice to an insistent whisper. "Whatever you do, don't get the I Can't Believe It's Not Buttercream icing. You will have no problem believing it's not butter."

"You ran all the way here to tell me that?"

"No," Mandy shook her head as she took a moment to catch her breath. "I've been tearing the station apart to tell you about Zayn."

Katie's stomach tightened. "What about him?"

Mandy looked over her shoulder at the two aliens and pulled Katie a few steps farther away. "He came to see me in the medical bay."

Katie remembered talking to Zayn the night before about the pains in his head. She also remembered a lot of other things, and her face warmed at the memory. "I told him he should come see you. He was worried about some pains he's been having."

Mandy nodded as if she already knew all that. "He should be worried."

"What do you mean?" She grabbed the woman by both arms. "Is he okay?"

"No. I mean, I don't know." Mandy bit down on the corner of her lip. "Listen, I could be wrong about all this." Her eyes darted to the aliens behind them and back to Katie. "I hope I'm wrong."

Katie gave her a small shake. "You need to calm down and tell me what the hell you're talking about. You're kind of freaking me out here."

Mandy let out a long breath. "I'm sorry. Like I told you, Zayn came in about his pains. He seemed nervous, so I told him I'd run some scans on him without bringing in the Drexian doctors or other medics."

"Thanks," Katie said, giving the woman's arm a light squeeze. "I'm sure that made him feel better."

"Yeah, well, that was before I found something odd when I scanned his head."

The tightness in Katie's stomach became a hard knot. "What do you mean by odd? Like a tumor?"

Mandy gave a curt shake of her head. "I don't think so, but again, I'm not a fully-trained medic yet, although using the medical scanners they have up here is a bit of a no-brainer." She took a shaky breath. "I saw something at the base of his brain stem on his spinal cord."

"Something like?"

"Like something that doesn't belong there," Mandy said. "I don't know if it's an implant or what, but it's not organic. Which doesn't make any sense, because he got a full check-up when he arrived at the station. They would have seen this."

Katie felt the tremor in her hands even as she held onto Mandy. "So what does this mean?"

"I don't know, but if the Kronock put it in there, and it has something to do with what's been going on all over the ship, I don't think it can be good," Mandy said. "I told Zayn I wouldn't tell anyone, but I can't keep this a secret for long, especially if it means everyone on this station is in danger."

Katie swallowed hard, wishing she hadn't tasted the weird cake samples. Everything had seemed so perfect last night. For the first time in as long as she could remember, she'd let down her defenses and let someone in. She'd trusted him and now he might end up being...what? A spy for the Kronock? An unwitting weapon?

She gave herself a mental shake. Whatever it was, she knew it wasn't his fault. He hadn't lied to her or played her. That was more than she could say for herself. She'd been playing everyone all along. She looked at the worried look in Mandy's face, and felt guilty about her plan to expose everyone who'd been so nice to her. She pushed that aside.

Right now, she needed to find Zayn before he tried to be a hero and do something stupid.

Chapter Twenty-Five

Z ayn stood on the balcony, breathing in the scent of the grass and focusing on the sound of a flock of small, white birds flapping their wings as they flew by. He'd wandered around the station for a while before finding himself back in the suite, although he barely remembered the walk.

Thoughts swirled through his mind. Was there really something in his head and, if so, how had the doctor missed it the first time? Was there any chance Mandy was lying to him? He shook his head. No, she'd been as shocked as him. She'd even done the scan three more times, each time the look on her face more grim.

He slammed a hand against the polished-wood railing. He wanted to destroy every Kronock who'd ever lived for doing this to him. But doing what, exactly? Mandy couldn't tell him what was in his head, or if it had anything to do with the ship malfunctions. But Zayn knew. The Kronocks were brutal and more strategic than the Drexians had given them credit for. His gut told him this was part of their scheme. He didn't know how, but they had made him part of their plan to invade and destroy.

Something clicked in his brain. Now it all made sense. It had been too easy to escape. Why had there been no other guards near the cells? He'd always heard several of them, but when he escaped the area was empty. He gritted his teeth. What he'd thought was good luck must have been planned all along so he could return to Drexian space with their device in his head.

"What are you?" he said, rubbing the back of his neck. It seemed clear that he was part of the ship's problems, but was that it? He couldn't imagine the Kronock would bother to send him back just to make lights flicker on and off. No, it was more deadly. He was more deadly.

"Zayn!" Katie's voice shattered the near-silence. She stood just inside the door, but it was clear from her heavy breathing that she'd run to get there.

He tried to smile, but he knew it was pointless to pretend. She knew. He could see it in the lines of concern etched on her face.

"Mandy told me everything." She walked to him, haltingly at first, then faster. When she reached him, she slipped her arms around his waist.

He felt her body trembling and wrapped his arms around her, the feeling of her softness comforting him. "I'm okay." It was a lie, but he didn't want to scare her any more than she already was.

Katie pulled back, her eyes wide. "It's not okay. What kind of monsters put something in your head?"

"The Kronock."

She let out a breath. "Yeah, I guess so. There really is nothing good about those guys, is there?"

He brushed a curl off her forehead. "Mandy shouldn't have scared you like she did. It could be nothing."

"Yes, she should have," Katie said. "I'm your…fiancé…or tribute bride or whatever. Anyway, she was right to tell me. So what are we going to do?"

Zayn tensed. "We can't keep this a secret for long. I know Mandy promised not to tell her mate right away, but it isn't safe to keep it from him or the captain for long. I'm not safe."

"Don't be ridiculous. You aren't dangerous." Katie pulled his chin down so his eyes met hers. "I know you. You wouldn't do anything to hurt anyone. Except maybe the Kronock and they *so* deserve it."

"Not on purpose," he said, "but if whatever is in my head is damaging the ship, then it isn't safe for me to be here. And if it's some sort of weapon…"

Katie fisted a hand in his shirt. "Don't say that."

Zayn stepped away from her, dislodging her hands from him. "It's true. Until we know what they did to me, I'm a danger to everyone on board, including you."

"So, what?" She put her hands on her hips. "You're going to leave the station?"

"If that's what it takes to keep you safe." He couldn't meet her eyes as he said it, the idea of leaving her making his chest ache.

"But we just…" Her words trailed off.

"I wouldn't be able to live with myself if I hurt you," he said, clutching the nape of his neck. "I'm supposed to protect you, but I can't do that as long as this thing is in my head."

"Then let's get it out," Katie said, grabbing his hand and tugging at it. "Aren't the surgeons up here supposed to be amazing? Mandy said the medical technology is wild. I can't imagine they couldn't get rid of one tiny device."

He jerked his hand. "Don't you think the Kronock thought of that? What if it has some sort of self-destruct if it's removed?"

Katie glanced at his head and her skin lost whatever color it had. "I didn't think of that." She tightened her grip on his hand. "I still think we should talk to the doctor before you run off without me."

He pulled her close, running his hands up through her curls and forcing him to meet his gaze. "I don't want to run off anywhere without you. I don't want to be without you ever again. Don't you know that?"

Color sprang to her cheeks. "I guess I do. It's just been so fast."

"That doesn't mean it's not real." He kissed her softly.

When he pulled away, she smiled up at him. "How do you still taste like doughnuts?"

He laughed and kissed her more deeply this time, feeling her sink into him. When they came up for breath, he brushed his thumb across her lower lip.

"I almost forgot," Katie said, pulling a silver capsule the length of her hand out of the slim side pocket of her pants. "Mandy wanted me to give you these. She said you ran out of the medical bay before she could give them to you. They're to help with the pains until we figure out how to stop them. She said they've got more kick than Pirrin tablets, so don't take one and drive heavy machinery. Like a space ship, I guess."

He took the capsule and heard pills rattling around inside. "Tell her thanks. She's not so bad, you know. Even if she is the reason you're up here."

Katie narrowed her eyes at him and grinned. "I know. Maybe instead of being mad at her for being the reason I'm up here, I should be thanking her."

"Maybe we both should," he said, wrapping his arms around her again.

As Zayn leaned down to kiss her, a pain knifed through his head and he dropped to one knee.

"What's happening? It's the pain again?" Katie asked, kneeling down beside him. "Is it worse than usual?"

He grasped the sides of his head with both hands, pressing his skull to try to stop the excruciating feel of a blade jabbing him over and over. The holographic scene around them disappeared, the lights flickered, and then the room went black. Instead of stopping, the pain intensified. Zayn rolled onto the floor, curling his feet up into his body.

"Zayn!" Katie groped at him in the dark, her hands as desperate as her voice.

The lights flashed back on, followed by the serene African savannah.

Zayn's head throbbed, and he felt a wave of nausea. He tried to push himself onto his knees, but dropped back to the floor as his stomach convulsed.

"I'm going to get help," Katie said, standing. "This is out of control."

"Wait." His word came out like a croak.

"If we don't do something this is going to kill you, and I refuse to watch you die if I can do something to save you." She ran toward the door. "Don't worry. I won't tell anyone else. I'll get Mandy."

He watched the door close, knowing she was right but wanting to stop her. The longer he could put off reality, the better. He knew finding out more about the implant would not make him feel better. He wished he could stay in the suite with Katie and pretend nothing was wrong for just a little while longer.

After a few minutes, he managed to stand, leaning against the railing to keep him steady. The pains were escalating; there was no denying it. He felt a burst of anger at the unfairness of it all. He'd wanted to die in the battle that had taken his unit, but he'd been kept alive. He'd wanted to return to battle, but he'd been given extended R&R. He hadn't wanted a tribute bride, but he'd been forced to accept one. Now that he'd fallen for her and finally felt deserving of someone so beautiful, she was going to be ripped away from him. If the Kronock had wanted to destroy him in a way more painful than death, they'd found it.

Zayn paced the room, the capsule of pills held tightly in his hand. He wanted to throw them across the room. What good were pills when he had an alien device in his head? He put a hand to the base of his spine, pressing down and trying to feel the thing. If only he could rip it out, he thought, his fingers digging into his flesh.

He strode to the far side of the bed and opened the drawer in the nightstand, tossing the sleek container of pills inside. As he started to close it, his eyes caught on some papers in the back. Sitting down, he pulled the drawer out all the way. There was a cocktail napkin, a folded sheet, and a blank notepad. He read the words written on the cocktail napkin. What were descriptions of the Boat doing on here?

He then unfolded the single sheet of paper. More notes about the station as well as details about Drexians, about him. This was clearly Katie's writing, but why was she writing all these things down? He flipped the sheet over and read the sentence at the top and felt like he'd been punched in the gut. She was drafting a story of some kind about being taken from Earth, but it was clearly written as if someone from Earth was reading it. He read the words "Back on Earth" along with a bulleted list of things to do that included 'pitch exposé to mag' and 'recover car.' The words *National Enquirer*, *Daily Star*, and *Entertainment Tonight* were scrawled in the lower corner. Was she planning to get this back to her planet somehow and expose everything?

He dropped the paper and it fluttered to the floor. Had everything she'd done been to get information from him? The relative ease with which she'd accepted the match, her eagerness to plan the wedding, the sexy dress, the romantic dinner? Had it all been for a story?

He crumpled the napkin and tossed it back in the drawer. Now it all made sense. She hadn't really been attracted to him, hadn't really cared for him. How could she? He'd known from the beginning that a pretty female would never fall for a damaged grunt like him. He'd been a fool to believe her.

Blood pounded in his ears as he stood and his head swam. He was wrong. This was worse than a punch in the gut. This was worse than being tortured. At least that had an end. This pain twisted his heart and threatened to never let go. He'd been wrong. So wrong. She was never his. It was all a lie.

He stumbled from the room, feeling more alone than ever.

Chapter Twenty-Six

Katie ran along the wooden walkway that stretched over turquoise water. They'd told her in the medical bay that Mandy was in her suite and had given her directions to the South Pacific wing.

If Katie hadn't been in such a rush, she would've stopped to stare. After passing through the automatic doors she'd been transported into a holographic environment that looked exactly like Tahiti. At least what she assumed Tahiti looked like. It wasn't like Katie had ever been. Actually, she'd never been anywhere outside the US except for a jaunt to Tijuana years ago with her father that had gone very badly.

She shuddered as she remembered almost landing in a Mexican prison. It had been the last job she'd pulled with her father. She shook the bad memories from her mind as she hurried down the path. Her shoes slapped against the wood, the only sounds aside from the water lapping against the white sand.

She reached the suite number they'd given her and knocked hard. She shifted from one foot to the other as she waited, hoping Mandy was there.

Katie didn't know who else to talk to, but she knew she needed to talk to someone. She tried to steady her breath as she rapped her knuckles on the door again. After running all the way to the medical bay and then all the way here, her breathing was heavy and uneven. She didn't want to appear hysterical to Mandy, even though the woman knew what was going on.

The door swished open, and a big Drexian with dark hair that fell around his neck stood in nothing but black uniform pants. His broad chest was bare and sweaty and his face flushed. Katie didn't know what to say. Maybe she'd gotten the wrong room?

She looked past him and saw Mandy hopping off the bed and slipping on a robe. Now she realized what she'd interrupted. "I'm so sorry. I came to talk to Mandy, but I can come back later."

Katie started to back away when Mandy appeared behind her husband in the pink silky robe. Her face broke into a smile. "Hey, there. I see you've met Dorn."

"Right," Katie said. "Dorn is your husband."

The man in question inclined his head at her. "You must be Katie."

"You know about me?" Katie asked.

"The human with bright-red hair who was taken as a tribute bride because of my wife?" He gave her a half smile. "I might have heard about you once or twice."

Mandy swatted at his big bicep. "I haven't talked about her that much. You'll have to forgive my husband. He likes to exaggerate."

"Drexians don't exaggerate," Dorn said.

"Whatever," Mandy said. "So what's up? I'm guessing you didn't come here just to meet Dorn."

Katie looked from Mandy to Dorn, unsure how to proceed. "I wanted to talk to you."

Mandy's eyes flared with understanding. "About that thing earlier?"

Katie nodded.

Mandy glanced at her husband and let out a breath. "I think we need to tell him."

Katie knew Mandy was right, but it still felt disloyal telling more people when she promised Zayn she wouldn't. She also knew he might not be thinking straight, especially since he had something implanted in his brain.

Dorn crossed his arms over his chest. "Tell me what?"

"I was going to tell you anyway." Mandy rested a slender hand on his forearm. "I wanted to give Katie a chance to talk to Zayn, first." She looked at Katie. "Did you find him?"

"I found him, and he told me the same thing you did. Then the power went out, and it was so painful he couldn't get up again. That's why I came to get you. I think it's getting worse."

"What's getting worse?" Dorn drummed his fingers against his arm.

"It's like this," Mandy said. "Zayn came to see me in the medical bay about some pains he's been having in his head. I didn't think too much about it since he'd gotten the okay from the doctors after he arrived here, and it seems normal to have residual pain after being tortured like he was. But when I scanned him, I found something. Something that definitely shouldn't be there."

Dorn narrowed his eyes. "Something that shouldn't be where?"

Mandy took a deep breath. "The scanner picked up some sort of device at the base of his brain stem. It's not organic, but I can't tell exactly what it is. And before you ask, I checked three times and used two different scanners just in case the first one was malfunctioning."

"The Kronock must have done it," Katie said. "That's the only explanation, except it doesn't make sense that the doctors didn't find it when they examined him here. If he hadn't been having pains every time the ship malfunctioned, he might never have gotten it checked again."

Dorn's face swiveled from Katie to Mandy. "So you're telling me that a Drexian warrior who was tortured and held prisoner by our enemy has been having a physical reaction every time the ship malfunctions, and no one thought to mention it until now?"

"They weren't as bad at first," Katie said. "At least, I don't think so. And it took a little while to realize the pains were coming right before the malfunctions and not at the same time, or after."

"So this device could be causing the malfunctions?" Dorn asked as he looked at his wife.

Mandy shrugged. "I have no idea. I think someone with a lot more knowledge about brains or technology would need to figure that out."

Dorn turned and strode across the room, snatching a dark shirt from the rumpled bed and pulling it on. "Where is he now?"

"I left him in our suite." Katie couldn't help peering into their suite at the glass panel in the floor that looked down into the ocean. It was like one of those overwater bungalows she'd heard about, the ones so popular with honeymooners and people with loads of money.

Dorn didn't slow as he walked past her out of the room and into the hallway. "Let's go."

Mandy gave a little yelp behind him. "Aren't you going to let me get dressed?"

He glanced back and winked at her. "You know I like you better without clothes."

Mandy pretended to be outraged, but Katie could tell that she loved it. She darted back into the room, running to the dresser at the far end, pulling out a yellow sundress and dropping the robe while she slipped it over her head. Even though she had on a pair of lace panties and a matching bra, Katie averted her eyes. Mandy ran back across the room and looped her arm through Katie's when she reached the door. "Okay, now we can go."

It didn't take long for them to leave the South Pacific wing and take the inclinator one level down to the Safari wing. Katie felt like a bundle of nerves. On the one hand, she was glad to have Dorn with them because he had the authority to help Zayn. On the other hand, she felt bad for telling him after promising Zayn that no one but Mandy would know his secret.

"We need to find out how this slipped by our medical team," Dorn said, over the soft instrumental Muzak of the inclinator. "After I talk to Zayn, I need to talk to the doctor who cleared him."

Mandy tugged at her bottom lip with her teeth. "I can't imagine how it happened. Drexian medical technology is so much more advanced than what we have on Earth. There is no way any doctor could have missed it. I mean, I caught it and I've only been training for a few weeks."

Dorn made a grunt of agreement. "Let's hope it's medical incompetence. Because if it's not, we're dealing with something much worse."

"What do you mean?" Katie asked, following the big man as he stepped off the inclinator and took long strides down the walkway of the Safari wing.

"I mean, if someone intentionally hid this, then we have a mole on the station."

Mandy sucked in air. "Like an enemy spy?"

"Or a Kronock agent of some kind."

Katie's stomach churned. "You don't think Zayn is a Kronock agent, do you?"

Dorn didn't say anything as they reached Katie's suite. "If he was, he wouldn't have told you about his pains, or gone to see Mandy. I suspect he's the victim in this scenario."

Katie swiped her hand across the panel in front of their door and stepped inside as it swished open. She expected to see Zayn still on the floor, or at least on the balcony, but he wasn't. Her gaze swept the room, but she didn't see him. She ducked her head into the bathroom. Empty.

Dorn took a few steps into the room and spun around. "He's gone."

"I don't know why he left," Katie said. "I told him I'd be right back with help." She pointed to a spot on the balcony. "He was curled up right there."

"Maybe he went for a walk," Mandy suggested, but her tone of voice told Katie she didn't believe her own words.

Katie walked past Dorn and pivoted to take in the entire room. Her gaze caught the open drawer of the bedside table, and she froze. Walking around the bed, she spotted the loose sheet of paper on the floor, and the cocktail napkin crumpled up inside the drawer. Her heart hammered in her chest. She knew now why he'd left. Dorn had found the notes she'd been taking for her exposé. Notes all about the Drexians, the space station, and him.

He knew she was a fraud.

Chapter Twenty-Seven

Zayn stumbled through the sleek modern corridors of the space station. He barely noticed passing a pair of Drexians in full uniform, or the cluster of human females giggling as they talked. His eyes were not drawn to the curved windows and the view of outer space. His mind reeled with what he'd discovered.

Had Katie been playing him all along? How long had she been taking notes about everything she saw on the station and all the things he told her? Since the first day? After they had been together? He scowled and kept his head down as he barreled along, trying not to think about how good it had felt to be inside her, how perfect everything it seemed when it was just the two of them in the bathtub.

It didn't matter now. Everything between them had been in his mind. He'd imagined that the looks she gave him meant something; that she cared for him as more than just the subject of her story. It had all been lies.

Zayn wasn't sure where he was going, but he needed to move. He'd had to get out of that room. The thought of being there when

Katie came back was unbearable. He couldn't stand to see her knowing that she'd been using him. He wasn't even angry with her. Not really. How could he expect someone like her to fall for a grunt like him? It wasn't her fault she been taken and matched with him. He didn't blame her for wanting to leave. But he also couldn't stand the thought of being without her.

He stopped and braced himself against the smooth wall, taking a heaving breath. Had he been walking in circles? He knew what he needed to do.

There was nothing keeping him on the station anymore, and every reason for him to leave. His presence was a danger to everyone on board, and to Katie. She may have broken his heart, but he still felt an overpowering urge to protect her. In his mind, she would always be his, the wild redhead with the soft, green eyes and the determined look. The last thing he wanted was something bad to happen to her. Especially if he could prevent it.

He turned around and made his way to the nearest inclinator, stepping on board and swiping his hand for the flight deck level. His leaving the ship would solve everyone's problems. There would no longer be a threat from his implant, Katie would not have to pretend to care about a damaged soldier like him, and he would not have to live with the guilt of hurting her.

He took long strides off the inclinator toward the flight deck, his boots echoing against the metal floor as he entered. A sense of calm settled over him as he scanned the ships and the raw metal space, breathing in the scent of burning fuel. He hadn't flown in a while, but he knew it would all come rushing back to him as soon as he got in the cockpit.

As he surveyed the various vessels available, a station-wide siren went off with red lights flashing overhead. He wondered if it was another malfunction, or if there was an incoming attack. When the transmission requesting all residents be on the lookout for him came across a loudspeaker, Zayn froze. An image of him was projected in the air holographically, and he recognized it as being the one taken of him when he'd enlisted. Even though it was a few years old, it still looked like him.

So much for leaving the station undetected, he thought. At least he was out of the corridors, where he'd be easily spotted. He ducked his head as he walked across toward a dingy shuttle. Better to take something low profile, than try to nab one of the fancy new fighters.

Before he could get on board he heard a voice calling his name. He turned out of habit.

"That's him," a Vexling in silver coveralls yelled, pointing at Zayn.

Zayn uttered a Drexian curse under his breath and bolted behind a row of metal drums. He heard footsteps pounding in his direction, and he kept running through the maze of shelving units until he reached a far door and ducked out and into the hallway. Luckily, it was devoid of people, and he ran until he reached a maintenance room, slipping inside and hiding behind a stack of metal crates. He'd have to wait until things cooled down to make his escape attempt again.

"I escaped from the Kronock. I'll escape from here, too," he muttered to himself, trying to suppress his fear that they'd let him go for a reason, and that the reason was implanted at the base of his skull.

Chapter Twenty-Eight

"**E**arth to Katie." The snap of Mandy's fingers brought Katie back to reality.

"Sorry about that." She crumpled the loose sheet of paper and cocktail napkins into her fists. "Just picking up some trash."

"So where do we think he went?" Mandy asked. "I thought you said the pain in his head had almost debilitated him."

Katie tried to shake off the regret that was consuming her, but it had become a cold ball in the pit of her stomach. "When I left him, he looked like he was in bad shape."

"Then he probably didn't go far," Dorn said. "Maybe he just wandered out looking for you."

"Maybe," Katie said, but she knew that wasn't the case. If Zayn had read her notes, then she doubted he was out looking for her. He probably wanted nothing to do with her.

She felt like she might throw up as the gravity of what she'd done hit her. Leaning over, her hands on her knees, she sucked in deep breaths. With her eyes closed, she could smell the faint scent of gardenia, and hear the animals moving slowly through the tall grass.

"It's not real," she said under her breath.

"What?" Mandy asked. "Are you sure you're okay?"

Katie wasn't okay. She was living in a fantasy world, and she'd destroyed the only real thing in it. Zayn was real and honest and brave, and she'd used him. Now he'd found out, and she knew he'd never look at her the same way again. The thought of that made her want to curl up into a ball.

Why did he have to find those notes? She wasn't going to use them. Not anymore. When she'd first decided to write the exposé and escape from the station, she'd barely known him. She hadn't known how kind he was and how much he seemed to care about her. It wasn't like she knew all that much about him now, but she knew the way she felt when she was with him, and how safe he made her feel. She didn't need to know every detail of his past to know that he was better than anyone she'd ever been with before.

But even with all that, she reminded herself, she'd still chosen to betray him. Maybe she just wasn't cut out to be with anyone. All those years with her dad conning people had taken their toll. Even when she cared about someone, she couldn't help but end up using them.

Katie straightened. Even if he hated her guts, he deserved her help. "I'm okay. I'm just worried."

Mandy rubbed her back. "Don't worry. I'm sure he's fine."

"Since we still don't know what we're dealing with, we need to find him." Dorn said, his green eyes narrowed with intensity. "The implant could just be harmful to him, or it could be a threat to the entire station."

"Should we split up and search for him?" Mandy asked.

Dorn shook his head. "I think you should go down to the medical bay and do a little digging. We need to know why the implant wasn't caught during his first exam, or if it was, who kept the information secret."

"I'll go with you," Katie said.

Mandy looked confused. "Don't you want to go look for Zayn?"

"Dorn knows the station better than I do," Katie said, trying to make her voice sound natural even though she heard the quaver and it. "I've only been to a few shops on the Promenade. I doubt he went there."

"Okay," Mandy said with a hesitant smile. "We'll go to the medical bay together."

Dorn gave a brusque nod. "And I'll check the flight deck on level two."

They left the suite, hurried down the walkway, and broke off into two directions. Katie noticed that Mandy turned to watch Dorn walk away and blew him a kiss. She pretended not to notice when Dorn winked at his bride and wagged his eyebrows suggestively, but the affection between the two made her heart ache.

Katie followed Mandy into the inclinator and let her swipe her hand over the panel to send them to the right level. She'd never been to the medical bay and wasn't even sure where it was located.

After descending several stories and twisting to one side, the inclinator doors slid opened, and Katie followed Mandy down the hallway to another set of double doors. She didn't know what she'd been expecting, but the wide room didn't look remarkably different from a hospital emergency room on Earth, that is, if you discounted the beds hovering in midair, and the squat robots zipping around at waist level.

"If anyone asks," Mandy said under her breath. "I'm checking you out for a stomachache. So try to look like you don't feel so well."

Katie nodded and clutched her stomach as Mandy led her to the end of the room and an empty bed.

"Hop up on there." Mandy grabbed a metal object from a levitating tray table and pressed a button to switch it on. It glowed green and beeped as she began waving it over Katie's midsection.

A siren went off overhead, sending flashing red light through the room. Mandy met Katie's eyes. "I guess Dorn really wants to find him."

Katie nodded, but couldn't speak for fear her voice would crack. She listened to the announcement alerting residents to watch for Zayn and studied the holographic image hovering in the air. It looked like him—the dark hair, the blue eyes—but it must have been taken before he was captured by the Kronock, because his expression wasn't haunted.

"Okay," Mandy said, louder than she needed to. "I'm just going to run this through the system." She dropped her voice to a mumble. "I'll be right back."

Katie tried to look believably ill as she sat on the hovering table. What was she doing? Why wasn't she going to look for Zayn? Because he wouldn't want to see her, the little voice in her head said. *He knows you're a fraud.*

Tears stung the back of her eyes. Why did he have to go and be so great and mess everything up? She was supposed to get her story, get off the station, and go back to her life on Earth. But now, all she could think about was the big Drexian with piercing blue eyes and scars on his arms. If she could get him back she wouldn't even care about going home.

"Do you require medical assistance?" a voice asked.

Katie glanced around her, seeing no one speaking. "Who was that?"

"I am Al, the virtual medical program. You appear to have an elevated heart rate. Would you like me to examine you for vascular irregularities?"

Katie glanced up, since the voice seemed to be originating from the ceiling. "So you're not real?"

"I am very real." If a computer program could sound offended, he did. "I have been programed with the combined medical knowledge of hundreds of species."

"Sorry," Katie said. "I'm from Earth. We don't have virtual doctors."

"I am aware of that fact," Al said. "My friend, Bridget, is also from Earth and told me of your primitive medical treatment."

Katie hesitated. "You're friends with Bridget?"

"Affirmative. She is the reason I am here and not still languishing on a deserted colony. You have not answered my question. Do you need medical attention?"

Katie swiped at her damp eyes as she saw Mandy walking briskly across the room toward her. "Thanks for the offer, but I'm okay."

"I see you met our medical AI," Mandy said, giving jerk of her head for Mandy to follow her. "We'll catch you later, Al."

Katie hopped off the bed as Al wished them both a good day in his halting voice. She let Mandy lead her out of the medical bay and into the hall.

"So?" Katie grabbed her by the arm to stop her rapid pace. "What did you find out?"

Mandy looked both ways, as if she was afraid someone would overhear her, but the hallway was empty. "I couldn't find the records of the original exam. They're gone."

"How can they be gone?" Katie asked. "Well, why don't we just ask the doctor who examined him?"

Mandy bit the edge of her thumbnail. "Well, that's going to be a problem, since he's not here anymore."

Katie shook her head. "I don't get it? What do you mean, he's not here anymore? Where is he?"

"Transferred to some outpost in the middle of nowhere. The day after he examined Zayn."

Chapter Twenty-Nine

Zayn crouched in the closet until the red lights stopped flashing. This was going to make getting off the station a bit more complicated. He wondered if Katie had alerted the station of his condition, or if Mandy had. He rubbed a hand across his face, feeling the slick sweat beading along his temples. It didn't matter now, although a part of him still desperately wanted it to have been Mandy and not Katie.

"Fool," he scolded himself under his breath. She'd already deceived him. Why did it matter if she'd betrayed his confidence?

He wanted to feel anger toward her. He wanted to feel rage. That, he could work with, channel into fuel. But this ache in his heart? The feeling that a part of him had been ripped out and he would never feel whole again? This did nothing but flood him with hesitation and doubt.

It didn't matter, he reminded himself, repeating the words in his head like a mantra. None of what he'd thought was real. None of the things he let himself imagine would happen, so he might as well get on with his plan.

Zayn peeked into the corridor and let out a sigh of relief. Empty.

The level with the flight deck and engineering was not the most heavily traveled, anyway. Only Drexian warriors and aliens working on ships needed to come here, so there wasn't the usual stream of Vexlings and Gatazoids and humans bustling around.

He walked quickly back to the flight deck and ducked in without being noticed. This time, he didn't take time to assess the ships, but slipped behind a stealth fighter in the middle of an overhaul. The bulk of the dark hull hid him well, and gave him a chance to watch the movement around him.

He'd almost decided on a stealth shuttle on the far side when a hand clamped down on his shoulder. Zayn spun and tried to land a punch to dislodge the grip, but he was dropped with a hard hit to his throat.

He lay flat on his back, his hands around his neck, as he tried to suck in air. "Grek, that hurt."

"I could have shattered your windpipe." Dorn stood over him, one arm extended.

Zayn took his hand and allowed himself to be heaved up. "Thanks, I think." His voice sounded hoarse. "How did you find me so quickly?"

Dorn shrugged. "I figured out where I'd go if I was in your situation, then I came here and waited for you to arrive."

"You knew I'd try to leave the station?"

"Like I said, it's what I would do if I thought I was a threat."

Zayn's hand went to the back of his neck, once again wishing he could rip the device out with his bare hands. "She told you?"

Dorn arched an eyebrow at him. "If by 'she' you mean my mate, then yes. But just so you know, your mate did not want her to."

Zayn felt a flutter of something in his stomach, but he shook his head. "It doesn't matter who told you. You know what I am."

Dorn studied him for a moment. "I know what they did to you, but none of us know what that means."

"It means they altered me, changed me, put something in me that does gods knows what." His voice rose as he spat out the words. "For all I know, this thing in my head makes me one of them."

Dorn pulled him by the sleeve and behind a shelving unit as heads began to turn their way. "You aren't Kronock. I know about the Drexian you saw when you escaped. My brother told me. But you aren't him. You are still a Drexian warrior."

Zayn raked a hand through his hair. "For now. How do I know this thing isn't set to switch on or detonate or activate me at some point? I could be a sleeper agent for the enemy without even knowing it. That's why I have to get off the station before I hurt anyone."

Dorn shifted from one foot to the other. "We should really examine you further. Maybe the medical team could determine what the device is."

Zayn met the other man's eyes. "That's your mate talking, not you. You know I have to do this. I'm too much of a risk to the everyone on board."

Dorn grunted but didn't respond. His pocket buzzed and he pulled out a small metal device, swiping a finger to illuminate a screen. He frowned as he read the text that appeared. "That's not good."

Zayn waited for him to look up, and then raised an eyebrow of his own.

"Mandy and Katie went to the medical bay to try to find the record of your original examination. Not only is it missing, but the doctor who examined you is no longer on the station."

Zayn's chest tightened at the sound of Katie's name, and he felt a small burst of hope that she was working with Mandy to help him. He tried to push all thoughts of her out of his mind and focus on what Dorn had told him. "What do you mean? Where is he?"

Dorn turned his attention back to the device. "He was sent to an output on the edge of nowhere the day after you were examined."

"So, someone on this station knew about this, about me?" So he'd been right. Sort of. Someone high up *did* want him to stay on the Boat for a reason. He wondered if they'd been the ones to ensure he got a tribute bride. It would make sense.

Dorn slipped the device back into his pocket and glanced over his shoulder. "This is bigger than just you, now. I don't know what's going on, but at least one person very high up knows, and has been covering it up."

Zayn folded his arms. "That doesn't change anything. I still need to get off the station. Maybe now more than ever. If whoever knows about this and has been trying to hide it realizes it's all about to fall apart, whatever the timeline is for this thing—" he said as he tapped his head, "—might be sped up."

Dorn looked at Zayn's head then away. "Agreed." He pulled the device back out of his pocket. "Do you want me to have Mandy bring your mate down here so you can talk to her?"

Zayn shook his head. "No. I don't want to see her before I leave." When he saw Dorn tilt his head at him curiously, he added, "I don't want to make it hard on her. Better if I just go."

"Okay. I can't admit to understanding human females, but don't you think she will be upset? Earthlings are much more emotional." His finger hovered over the screen. "Are you sure?"

"I'm sure."

Dorn put the device away and took Zayn's arm. "I'll authorize your departure, but only right before you're about to leave. We don't want to tip off the Kronock agent."

"Agreed."

The two men strode toward a ship with a sleek, black hull. Dorn leaned on a panel to release the hatch. "It's one of the transport vessels used to retrieve the tribute brides. It's got jump capability, of course, and stealth technology, but the weapons aren't much."

"Won't you get some heat for letting me take this?" Zayn asked.

"Not when I explain," Dorn said. "We have a few anyway. I thought you should take something larger than a shuttle in case you need to…"

"Live in it for a while?" Zayn finished the man's sentence as he peered inside the transport ship, realizing this would be his home for a while. It was a far cry from the luxurious suite he'd been occupying for the past few days, and he felt a stab of longing for what he was leaving behind.

"It's not the Boat, that's for sure," Dorn said, seeming to read his mind. "But it's got the basics: rations, bunks, medical supplies."

"It's more than I deserve."

Dorn grabbed his arm. "None of this is on you. As soon as we get this figured out, we'll get you back here and reunited with your bride."

Zayn shook off Dorn's arm and shook his head. "I'm not coming back."

"I don't understand. I know it's hard to adjust to taking an Earth female for a mate, but trust me when I say they grow on you."

"She doesn't want me," Zayn said, not looking at Dorn when he spoke.

"You're su—?"

"Positive." Zayn started up the ramp leading into the transport ship and turned.

Dorn stared at him, then sighed. "I'm going to need to create a distraction to get you out without being detected. Wait for my transmission before leaving."

Zayn gave a single nod before disappearing into the cockpit. "Tell her I'm sorry."

Chapter Thirty

"So, what do we do now?" Katie asked as she and Mandy hurried along the corridor. "Without the doctor or the initial medical report, we don't know who is covering this up or why."

"I wondered why one of the medical crew disappeared," Mandy said. "I never guessed he'd been sent away to cover up something."

"Do you know where he went? Maybe we could contact him. Are there interstellar phones up here? How do you get messages to people far away?"

Mandy smiled at her. "There are communication systems, but sometimes there can be a time delay depending on the distance and interference."

They got on the open inclinator with a Vexling male in a light-blue jumpsuit. Katie waited until the doors closed before she whispered to Mandy. "So where are we going?"

"I don't know," Mandy whispered back. "I'm trying to think what to do next. We should probably find Dorn."

Her communications device vibrated and she pulled it out of her pocket. Her eyes grew large as she read it, but she put it away without saying anything. The inclinator glided to a stop and the Vexling disembarked with a nod to both of them.

Once the doors slid shut again, Mandy spun toward her. "It's Zayn. Dorn found him."

"Really?" Katie's heart beat faster. "Is he with him? Let's go."

Mandy placed a hand on each of Katie's arms. "He's gone."

"Who's gone? Zayn? I thought you just said Dorn found him."

"He did, but Zayn convinced him that it would be safest if he left the station. Dorn got him on a ship and snuck him off."

"He left?" Katie heard the crack in her voice. "Just like that? Is this for good, or is he coming back?"

Mandy's blue eyes shone with tears as she looked at Katie. "I don't know. I guess until they can figure out what's going on with the implant and if it's dangerous."

"But if it's dangerous, then Zayn is all alone out in space with that thing in his head and no one to help him." Katie felt lightheaded as she thought of him voluntarily leaving by himself to ensure the safety of everyone else.

"I'm really sorry," Mandy said. "I know you were falling for—"

Katie waved a hand to cut her off. "I barely knew him, so don't worry about me." Even as she said the words, she knew they were lies. She may not have known him for long, but she knew his heart. She'd seen him anguish over his lost team, worry about her, and now sacrifice himself to protect her and an entire station.

"You don't mean that." Mandy's voice was soft, and made Katie's eyes burn with tears.

She looked up at the ceiling and tried to blink them away. "You're right. I don't. I'm just angry he left."

"He should have said goodbye, but I guess he was worried about getting off the station before anything else happened."

Katie knew why he'd left without seeing her, and that was what hurt the most. He hadn't wanted to see her again. If he read all her notes, he must have suspected that she'd been playing him all along, that none of it was real. A sob caught in her throat as she imagined how alone he must have felt when he realized the person he'd thought cared about him—the person he'd confided in and opened up to—was just using all his pain for a story. Zayn must have been relieved to get off the station and ensure that he'd never see her again, even if it meant a possible death sentence.

"I think I need to be alone," she said. "Do you mind if I go back to my suite?"

"Of course not." Mandy swiped a hand to send them to the African Safari level. "Why don't you rest for a while? I need to get a message to my brother-in-law, anyway."

"Dorn's brother?" Katie tried to remember the connections between everyone she'd met. "And Bridget's husband?"

Mandy nodded. "He's on assignment, but since he's with Drexian military intelligence, I thought he might be able to help us track down the doctor."

Katie nodded, but she felt numb. She knew Mandy and Dorn were worried about a wider plot, and what the implications were for the station and the Drexians in general. Katie couldn't get past the fact that Zayn was the pawn in all of it. He was being used by the Kronock, and he'd been used by her.

She swallowed the lump in her throat. She'd never meant to hurt him, but she hadn't been able to help herself. She'd seen an opportunity to get information to use for her own benefit and her lifetime of training had kicked in. By the time she'd realized that she had feelings for him and cared about him more than she cared about getting away and telling the story, it was too late. She'd ruined everything, and now Zayn was gone.

Even if he survived, she doubted he'd return to the station. The only reason he'd had was her, and she'd betrayed him. No, she'd seen the last of her big, Drexian warrior. He would never forgive her, and she didn't blame him.

The doors of the inclinator swept open, and Mandy gave her a final quick squeeze. "I'll let you know if I find out anything that could help Zayn. Try not to worry too much. Dorn and Kax are pretty resourceful. If anyone can get Zayn out of this, it's them."

Katie tried to return her smile, but her heart wasn't in it. Even if they saved Zayn, he wouldn't want her, and she didn't blame him. She waved as the doors closed on Mandy, and she trudged down the wooden pathway to her suite, ignoring the breathtaking scenery.

The sight of the birds swooping low and the grasses rustling made her want to scream. It wasn't real. None of it was real. It was more smoke and mirrors. She was sick of the pretense. Katie kicked one of the railings. The only thing that had been real was Zayn. The way he touched her, the way he looked at her. That had been real. She'd felt it in her core.

"Well, you messed that up real good," she muttered to herself as she reached her door. She thought about what was on the other side. The suite where she'd first met Zayn, the balcony where they'd talked, the bed where he'd made her feel things no man ever had, the bath…Her face burned as she thought about the way she'd felt with him, and then the tears rolled down her cheeks when she thought about how she'd destroyed it all.

"I can't do this," she said, turning away from the room. "I can't stay here without him."

She almost ran down the walkway to the inclinator. She didn't care about her story anymore. As a matter of fact, she had no desire to expose the Drexians, or their space station, or the tribute bride program. She didn't want to hurt anyone else, but she also knew she couldn't stay there. Not without Zayn. She had to get off the station and get back to Earth.

Katie hurried onto the inclinator car as the doors opened, not meeting the eyes of a Gatazoid with a hover cart covered with silver domes. She waited until he disembarked to select the floor for the flight deck, remembering that Dorn had said it was on level two. She didn't want anyone to be able to track her movements until she was safely back on Earth.

As the inclinator dropped, Katie thought about Mandy and Reina. They would be upset when they found her missing, but she hoped they'd understand. She figured Serge would be hysterical until he was given another wedding to plan. The only other person who would miss her presence was probably light years away from her by now.

This was for the best, she told herself, as she stepped out of the inclinator and looked both ways down the wide corridor. This part of the station was less sleek and shiny. The lighting was not as bright, and the hallways didn't boast a spectacular view of space. She suspected this was because tribute brides never visited this level. Aside from when they first arrived, and at that time they were all unconscious. Hard to believe that had only been a few days ago.

Katie spotted a Drexian in a black flight suit exit a wide doorway down one side and she walked purposely in that direction, glad the warrior didn't turn and see her. The doors slid open as she approached, and she faltered for a moment. The space was massive, stretching across what she suspected was the width of the entire station. Space ships of various sizes were scattered across the dull metal flooring, some in the process of repairs, and others being loaded up with supplies. She noticed a line of black fighters, their noses long and their wings curved.

She needed to move fast and find one of the ships that brought tribute brides from Earth. They would have to be larger than fighters or shuttles, since they were equipped with facilities to carry more than one female at a time, and she suspected they traveled with a small crew. Her eyes rested on pair of black ships that were clearly transports. Bingo. They were the only ships that looked large enough and had the black stealth paneling she'd heard about.

Katie edged her way around the room, trying not to draw attention to herself. Luckily, the crew seemed too preoccupied by their work to notice her ducking behind crates and scooting around barrels. One of the transports had its hatch open, so she walked briskly up it, not looking left or right or slowing down until she was inside the ship. She heard the engines power up and the hatch begin to rise as she slipped into the back. Her heart pounded as the ship shuddered and started to move across the flight deck. She'd made it just in time.

Katie knew she should find a place to hide for the flight, so she opened a door and saw a trio of pod-shaped beds with clear lids. She assumed that was how she'd arrived on the station, but she had no desire to climb in one now. Her stomach lurched as the ship increased its speed, and she was knocked off her feet at what was likely takeoff. She hit the wall and gave a small yelp, startled by the jolt of the ship and the impact against her shoulder.

She rubbed her arm and hoped no one heard her. All she needed to do was keep hidden until they reached Earth in a little less than two hours. Then, she could sneak off the ship while the Drexians went off to gather the new crop of tribute brides.

"Easy, peasy," she whispered to herself, looking around the room for a closet she could hide in. She didn't see anything, so she began opening the lower cabinet doors. There was always a chance she could squeeze in under there.

"What do you think you're doing?" The voice made her jerk around and yelp again.

Katie felt like the air had been knocked out of her, as she looked up at the towering Drexian, his blue eyes flashing with anger and shock.

"Zayn?"

Chapter Thirty-One

"I asked you what you think you're doing?" Zayn's voice was a low rumble, and he saw her flinch as he stared down at her.

He didn't know if he was more surprised to see Katie rummaging around in the cabinets, or angry that she'd stowed away on his ship. The whole purpose of him leaving was to keep her safe, and here she was. Another part of him—maybe the biggest part—wanted to pull her into his arms and never let go. Then he remembered all her notes and the secrets she'd been keeping. "Well?"

"What are you doing here?" Her voice cracked when she finally spoke. "Dorn told me you'd already left the station."

So she hadn't been trying to stow away with him. He felt his spark of hope flicker out. She'd just been trying to leave. "I had to wait until he could create a distraction on the bridge so my departure wouldn't be detected. He doesn't know who the Kronock agent is, so he can't trust anyone." He took a step closer. "I guess you're just trying to get back to Earth so you can tell everyone about us, right? Isn't that why you were taking notes? And those names in the corner. Is that where you plan to sell your story?"

He heard the anger in his voice and watched her cower. He backed away, ashamed of himself for scaring her. "It doesn't matter anymore."

She opened and closed her mouth a few times, her cheeks as red as her hair and her eyes swimming with tears. "It does matter. I'm not writing a story. I was at first, but that was before…"

He felt his heart knocking in his chest. His hurt and fear and anger were all mixed up together, and even though he wanted to trust her, he couldn't. Not again. "You want me to believe you changed your mind? Then why are you on a transport?"

Her eyes went to the floor. "You're right that I'm trying to get back to Earth. I'm not going to lie to you anymore."

He gave a bitter laugh. "You've been lying to me from the beginning, haven't you? Why should I believe you now?"

"It wasn't all lies," she said, reaching a hand out to him. "What I felt when I was with you wasn't a lie."

Her touch sent a jolt through him, and he clamped his own hand over hers. "How do I know that?"

"Can't you feel it?" Katie closed the distance between them and pressed her other hand to his chest. "You can't fake something like this."

His pulse quickened and blood rush to his cock as her body brushed up against his. He wanted to stay angry with her and let her feel a bit of the pain he felt, but his body betrayed him.

Zayn backed her up until she hit the wall. He kept pressing until his body was grinding against hers. "I have never faked what I've felt for you. Even when I knew that I didn't deserve you and should walk away, I couldn't hide my feelings."

"I'm the one who doesn't deserve you," she said as tears rolled down her cheeks. "I was a coward. I've never felt this way before and it scared me, so I told myself that I was doing it all for my story. That was the real lie."

He brushed her tears away with the his thumbs, feeling her body trembling. "No more lies."

She shook her head. "I thought I'd never see you again. That's why I got on the transport. I didn't want to stay on the station without you."

"I left to keep you safe. I'd rather die than let anything happen to you," he said with a husky laugh. "So much for that."

She lifted her arms and ran her hands through his hair, her eyes studying his face as if she was memorizing it. "I don't care what happens. As long as I'm with you."

Zayn crushed his mouth to hers, all anger melting away as he felt her body responding to him and heard her breathy sigh. He didn't care about the past anymore, and he couldn't even think about the future. All that mattered was the two of them in that moment, and knowing that she was his. The blood pounded through his body as his hands wrapped around her, grabbing her soft, round ass and lifting her up. She wound her legs around his waist and moaned in his mouth.

"I need you," she gasped, when she'd pulled away.

He looked at her pink cheeks and her wild hair, her green eyes burning with desire. He captured her face in one hand, rubbing his thumb across her wet bottom lip. "Tell me you're mine."

"I'm yours, Zayn. I always have been." She took his thumb into her mouth and sucked it hard, and his eyes rolled up nearly into the back of his head.

The desire to claim her slammed through him. He pressed her back against the wall and reached down, stripping her pants off her and tearing away the flimsy lace panties. He saw her pupils flare as he tugged his own pants down and his cock sprang free. With one hand, he dragged his crown through her wet folds. She was so wet and hot his knees almost buckled. "I can't be slow this time." The words came out through gritted teeth. "I need to take you hard. Need to claim you."

She nodded quickly, her eyes locked with his. "I'm yours. Take me hard."

He thrust himself into her, feeling her tightness like a glove as he stroked deep. Katie cried out as he pounded again and again, her eyes never leaving him.

"That's right," he said. "It's my cock that's inside you, Katie. Do you like that?"

"So good," she gasped. "I love when you're inside me."

"You need it, don't you?" He leaned down and kissed her, his tongue swirling with hers before pulling away and leaving her breathless. "Tell me." He thrust harder. "Tell me what you need."

Her eyes were wide, and she was panting as her head bobbed up and down. "I need you, Zayn. I need your cock filling me."

He looked down to where their bodies joined and watched himself stroking inside her. "You're so tight where I split you."

She rolled her head back. "I'm so full with your cock."

She was his, and every deep thrust claimed her as his. Her throaty moans belonged to him and every one of her sweet releases were his to savor. He angled her body so he rubbed against her clit, and she clutched at his shoulders, moving her hips frantically as she began to quiver. He felt his release building as her muscles clamped around him. "Come for me, Katie. Only for me."

"Only you," she panted.

Zayn grabbed her by the hips and slammed up into her as he felt her orgasm sending her over the edge, her screams melding with his as he pulsed into her, his pleasure almost blinding as he held himself inside her throbbing heat.

Katie's entire body shook as her legs went limp and slipped from his waist. He caught them and kept himself from falling by bracing one hand against the wall.

"I sure am glad I got on the wrong ship," she said, her words escaping between ragged breaths.

Before Zayn could respond, the ship jerked to one side. He staggered a few steps but caught himself before falling.

"What was that?" Katie asked, dropping her legs to the ground so she could stand.

"I don't know." He pulled his pants up and bolted for the cockpit.

Katie followed behind, tugging her pants back on. She stopped short when she reached the cockpit and saw the huge ship hovering in front of theirs. "What is that?"

"A Kronock battleship." Zayn's chest constricted as he sat down and began flipping switches. "They must have been tracking me."

"Don't we have that Drexian stealth technology? How can they see us?"

All the happiness that Zayn had felt moments ago had evaporated and now formed a pit in his stomach. "It must be the device. They don't need to see the ship if they know I'm right here."

"Can we outrun them?" Katie asked, her voice shaky. "Fly away at light speed?"

"They'll follow." Zayn slammed his hand against the console. "I was supposed to draw the danger away from you. Not draw you into danger."

She put a hand on his shoulder. "I wouldn't want it any other way."

He swiveled around to face her. "I won't let them take us prisoner. I won't let you suffer like that."

"I understand." Her face was grim as she sat down on his lap and looped her arms around his neck. "You're still trying to protect me."

"Always," he said, hearing his own voice thick with emotion.

From the corner of his eye, he saw a red flash coming from the enemy ship. He instinctively rolled Katie under him as he dove to the floor and the ship was rocked from the impact. He kept his arms around her as they were flipped over and over, the instrument panels screaming out warnings and emergency lights flashing.

Zayn heard the deafening sound of air leaving the ship and knew there was a breach. The emergency functions immediately sealed the breach, but the ship continued to flip end over end, bouncing them around the cockpit. When they came to a stop, Zayn felt like he'd gone ten rounds in a holographic fighting ring with his hands tied behind his back.

"Are you okay?" he managed to say, running his hands up and down Katie's body to feel for any injuries.

"I think so." She sounded dazed as she blinked up at him. "What happened?"

He pulled them both to standing. The red warning lights flashed and the console still wailed, and Zayn smelled something burning. He looked out the view screen. No Kronock ship. Either they'd been knocked so far they were out of visual range, or the enemy had left. He staggered to the controls and assessed the damage. They'd lost both engines and suffered a major hull breach. Not good.

He glanced at a red flashing light and tapped the screen. That couldn't be right. His breath caught in his throat as he looked again. Now he knew why the Kronock had left them. The impact had damaged their life support systems.

They had less than ten minutes before they ran out of air.

Chapter Thirty-Two

Katie just blinked at Zayn a few times after he told her. "Life support as in oxygen? We're going to run out of oxygen?"

"I'm so sorry." His eyes dropped to the console and the flashing lights.

She felt a calm settle over her. "It's not your fault. None of this is your fault."

He gave a quick shake of his head without looking up. "If I'd never escaped and come to the station, you wouldn't be floating out in space running out of air."

She put a finger under his chin and lifted his face. "Then I never would have met you. I'd take this ending to that alternative."

He pulled her into his lap and buried his head in her neck. "I don't deserve you."

She stroked the back of his neck. "You're really going to have to stop saying that. I'm the one who doesn't deserve you. You wouldn't be so impressed with me if you knew what I was like on Earth."

Zayn raised his eyes to hers. "There's nothing you can tell me that would change the way I feel about you. Don't you know that?"

She took a shaky breath. "You weren't the first person I deceived. Not by a long shot. You see, I grew up with a father who made a living by conning people." When she noticed his brows furrow, she explained. "He would run cons to trick people out of their money. Everything he did was a deception. He taught me how to manipulate and trick and lie. It was all I knew, and I hated it. I tried to get away from the business, but even then the best job I could find was taking pictures of famous people and exploiting them. I didn't get close to anyone because I was taught to never trust anyone. Every guy I ended up getting involved with was either a cheat or a loser. It was like I was a magnet for bad people no matter how much I tried to escape my past."

"When I look at you, I don't see any of that," Zayn said, brushing a curl off her face. "I see the woman who didn't judge me for having nightmares and who listened to me talk about my guilt and pain. You made me feel safe after my world had been destroyed, and you never made me feel like just a scarred soldier."

Katie's eyes welled up with tears. "I guess I didn't feel like I was one to judge anyone. None of the horrible things that happened to you were your fault. You didn't deserve to be tortured or have something put into your head. Like I said, I always had a soft spot for underdogs. That's why I could never be a real con artist like my father. I felt too bad for the people he victimized."

"You aren't your father."

She took a shallow breath. "And you're more than just a soldier with scars." She kissed him lightly. "You're a Drexian warrior, and you're all mine."

"And you're mine." His eyes drooped as he pulled her face to his.

Katie head swam as he kissed her, and she wasn't sure if it was the emotions of the moment, or the waning oxygen. When she pulled away, she let her head sink onto his shoulder. "I wish we had more time. I would have liked getting to be your mate."

Zayn wrapped his arms around her, tugging her closer. "You already are my mate. I don't need a ceremony to know you're mine."

"Neither do I," Katie said, smiling at him even though her head had started to ache. "To be honest, I was never crazy about the idea of a big wedding. It seems a little silly to me. I don't need a ring or a fancy dress or a marriage certificate to know that my heart belongs to you."

He kissed her again, his tongue parting her lips and delving deeper. She sank into the kiss, savoring the taste of him.

"Still tastes like doughnuts," she said with a giggle when they'd stopped. She wanted to run her hands through Zayn's hair, but her arms felt heavy and sluggish. "I love the way you taste and feel and smell." She sank into him, feeling almost giddy. "I love all of you."

"I love you." His voice sounded deeper and slower than usual.

She felt his arms go slack around her. A part of her knew they were close to the end, but she couldn't seem to care about it. She felt so good sitting on Zayn's lap, her head slumped against his chest inhaling the warm scent of him. At least she was with the man she loved, she thought. Her brain felt jumbled, but that thought was clear. She loved him. As absurd as it seemed, especially for someone like her who didn't really believe in love, she'd fallen for him. What had first been lust had deepened as her feelings were tested and she'd seen how honorable and loyal he was.

"No regrets," she whispered, her breaths tiny gasps.

He kissed the top of her head gently. "No regrets."

It wasn't so bad, Katie thought as her eyes fluttered closed. There were worse ways to go. She would have liked more time, but at least she'd been able to tell Zayn everything. She wouldn't have been able to live with herself if he'd never known how she felt about him. A single tear trickled down her cheek, although she didn't feel sad.

Her mind flashed to the two of them in their suite, and then of sitting in the bathtub with him, the bubbles up around her neck. She could almost feel the warm water and smell the flowery bath oils and see the glow of the candles. She tried to hold onto the memory, but the glow of the candles grew brighter, blocking out everything else. The candles were almost blinding. She frowned and tried to open her eyes, but all she could see through the slit of her eyelids was a light shining through the ship's window.

If she hadn't been so drowsy she might have wondered who was out there and why she heard her name and Zayn's being repeated over and over.

Chapter Thirty-Three

Zayn rolled his head to nuzzle in Katie's neck and felt his cheek touch something cold. He forced himself to open his eyes. He was not in the transport ship, and Katie was no longer sitting on his lap. He stared up at a white ceiling that looked vaguely familiar. He took a breath and the sharp scent told him he was in the medical bay on the Boat.

He tried to sit up, but his head felt heavy. He lifted a hand and touched thick bandages covering his forehead.

"Whoa there, buddy."

He recognized that voice, as well. It wasn't Katie's, but it was female.

Mandy's face came into view above him, her long, brown hair pulled up in a ponytail. "We wondered when you'd be joining us."

"Where's Katie?" His voice was little more than a croak, and his throat felt dry and scratchy.

Mandy put a hand on his shoulder as he tried to sit up again. "Don't try to move. You're still healing from your surgery. But don't worry, Katie's fine."

He relaxed, but then felt confused again. "What surgery?"

"We were able to remove that device from your spinal cord," Mandy said, then grinned. "Well, when I say 'we,' I don't mean I did it. I'm a long way from performing brain surgery."

"She means me," a robotic voice said.

"The AI cut me open?" Zayn instinctively raised a hand to his head. "It didn't detonate?"

"Of course it did not detonate." AI sounded indignant. "My skills as a surgeon are unsurpassed. I would never detonate a bomb in a patient, even the ones who talk too much."

"And there's that famous bedside manner," Mandy muttered.

"It didn't detonate because it wasn't a weapon." This voice was not Mandy's or AI's. Zayn turned his head slightly to see Dorn walking up. "I was able to get a message to Kax, who was able to track down the doctor who'd originally examined you and been sent off the station. He told my brother that he'd determined the device was a transmitter of some kind that was sending out energy pulses."

"So it was just meant to disrupt the ship?" Zayn asked.

"Looks like it, although enough system disruptions would have left the station vulnerable when the Kronock attacked, so it wasn't harmless." Dorn clasped his hands behind his back. "We're just lucky our enemy wasn't able to design a weapon to implant in you."

Zayn nodded, not sure if lucky was the word he'd use for what he'd been through. "Did you discover who hid the information and sent the doctor away from the station?"

Dorn's expression darkened. "Not yet. The doctor submitted his report to High Command, so it has to be someone on there, but the doctor had no idea who ordered his transfer. I checked the records, and they've been wiped."

"So someone on the High Command is behind this and is covering their tracks?" Zayn asked. "You know, I thought it was unusual that I was being held at the station and given a tribute bride, and now I know I was right to be suspicious."

"Looks like your instincts were correct." Dorn lowered his voice as he cast a glance over his shoulder at the others in the medical bay. "It's hard to imagine someone from one of the elite Drexian families would be an agent of our enemy, so I have to tread carefully. I need to be positive before I make an accusation." He blew out a breath. "At least, that's what my older brother tells me."

"I don't know why you're so shocked," Mandy said. "Politicians from elite families are the most corrupt people on our entire planet."

"Drexians are not Earthlings," Dorn growled.

"You could have fooled me," Mandy muttered, winking at Zayn and running a scanner over his head.

Zayn watched Dorn glower at his wife before she turned and fluttered his eyelashes at him. Dorn cleared his throat and his cheeks reddened, but he clearly couldn't help smiling at Mandy.

"Earth women will drive you crazy," Dorn told him. "Don't say I didn't warn you."

"Katie." Zayn's mind flashed back to being on the transport ship with her as they ran out of air. "She's okay after losing so much oxygen?"

"I promise you she's fine," Mandy said. "You two were without oxygen for less than a minute before Dorn's ship honed in on Katie's tracker and rescued you both."

Zayn shifted his attention to the Drexian. "You came after me? How did you know?"

Mandy sidled up to her mate and slipped an arm around his waist. "It was actually me. Katie told me she needed time alone in her suite, but I decided she shouldn't be alone after all and went to look for her. When I didn't find her, I suspected she might have done something drastic so I told Dorn. He activated her tracking device and discovered she was on your ship."

"Then I should thank you both."

"Zayn!" Katie flew through the doors of the medical bay and ran across the room to him, throwing herself across his chest. Her mass of red curls tickled his skin, which he just realized was bare to the waist. He stroked her head as she held him, and only when he felt her body shake did he realize she was crying.

He pulled her up and saw the tears running down her cheeks. "Why are you crying?"

"I'm so happy you're okay." She climbed up beside him in bed and curled her body next to his.

Dorn met his eyes, raising his eyebrows in a clear "I told you they were crazy" look. Mandy grabbed her husband by the elbow and dragged him away, waving at the two as she marched Dorn out of the medical bay.

"I'm relieved *you're* okay," he said, tilting her face up to his. "You were getting pretty loopy right before we were rescued."

She gave him a playful swat. "Was not. I meant every word I said to you, including the fact that you taste like doughnuts."

"Oh?" He leaned down and kissed her, feeling a surge of happiness that everything he'd remembered had been real. "Well, I meant every word I said to you too."

"Do you remember it?" Katie asked. "The rescue, I mean?"

Zayn thought back. "I remember a light and hearing a ship latch onto ours. But I don't remember the trip back to the station, or anything else, up until I woke up a little while ago."

Katie ran a hand down the side of his face. "They rushed you to surgery as soon as we got here. Dorn was talking to his brother and got the okay from the doctor to take out the device. They wanted to get it out before it could do any more damage." Her eyes went to the bandages. "Does it hurt?"

Zayn gave a small shake of his head. "I'm too happy to be with you to feel any pain."

She kissed him, her lips soft and her touch tender. "Well, we're still going to have to take it easy for a while."

"What does that mean?" He felt the blood course hot through his body in response to her touch.

She sat up and narrowed her eyes at him. "What do you think it means? You just had something taken out of your head." Her eyes went to the blanket around his waist and the growing bulge beneath it. "We're going to have to go slow."

Zayn ran one hand up her back and captured her head in his palm. He pulled her in for a long, deep kiss. "I can do slow."

Katie cleared her throat. "I'm not sure if that's what the doctor had in mind."

"I hope not." Zayn traced a finger down her throat to the dip in her cleavage. "I would not want any doctor to have in his mind what I'm planning to do to you."

She pushed herself off his chest as she looked over her shoulder. "Zayn!"

"What?" He gave her a look of complete innocence. "There is nothing wrong with a Drexian wanting to do these things with his mate." The pupils in his blue eyes widened. "And you are my mate. Now and forever."

"About that," Katie said. "I know when we were on the transport we said we didn't want a wedding."

"You did not mean it? You would prefer a big wedding?" He ran a hand through some loose curls falling over her forehead. "Whatever you want is fine with me. As long as you are happy."

"No, I meant it, but I know we need to have some sort of ceremony to formalize everything." Katie licked the tip of her tongue along her bottom lip. "But I have an idea I think you'll like."

A low growl escaped his throat as he watched her wet her lip. "I already like it."

Chapter Thirty-Four

"So Serge knows nothing about this?" Mandy asked Katie, as she straightened the lace swish train behind her.

Katie ran her hands down the length of the form-fitting ivory dress and studied her reflection in the bathroom mirror. "Not unless Monti and Randi spilled the beans."

Mandy shook her head. "I told them not to tell him I picked up the dress early upon pain of death. They remember helping me find a dress, and from the looks on their faces, they took me seriously."

"Good." Katie took a sip of the pink bubbly sitting on the marble countertop, grateful the sweet drink was helping calm her nerves. "I know Serge was hoping we'd move forward with the wedding planning, but with everything that happened, we just couldn't. A fancy wedding isn't either of our styles anyway."

"Don't worry about him." Mandy picked up her own glass of bubbly, taking a swig. "He'll get over it, eventually."

"Are we talking about Serge?" Bridget asked, as she joined the women in the bathroom, holding a swath of tulle in the air.

"You know it," Mandy said, taking the tulle and handing her the champagne flute in exchange. She eyed the pile of curls on Katie's head. "On the top or on the back?"

"The back," Katie said. "Zayn likes my curls."

Mandy slid the comb into her hair and fanned out the veil behind her. "One more thing." She grabbed a metal bottle and spritzed something on the veil.

"Is that hairspray?" Katie asked coughing from the smell.

Mandy nodded. "It keeps the veil in place."

Bridget laughed. "And you learned this…?"

"Being an Instagram influencer gave me some skills," Mandy said, making a face at her friend. "I could also take a fierce selfie, if there were any smartphones up here."

Bridget shook her head and turned her focus to Katie. "You look amazing. Zayn is going to be blown away."

Katie felt a flutter in her stomach and took another gulp of bubbly. "How is he?"

"Great," Bridget said. "Nervous. It's cute."

"Nervous like he wants to get the first shuttle off the station?" Katie asked.

Bridget put a hand on Katie's arm. "Nervous about being dressed up in front of so many people, I think, but Dorn's with him and distracting him by talking about warrior stuff."

"I'm sorry Kax couldn't come back." Katie met the woman's brown eyes. "Please tell him again how grateful we are for what he did."

"Are you kidding? He got to track down the doctor and discover how to disable the device and save a fellow Drexian. He lives for that stuff."

"I know Dorn would change places with him in a heartbeat," Mandy said. "Although tracking your ship and getting you both off before life support failed was enough of a rush to hold him for a while."

"I take it he'd rather be on assignment?" Katie asked.

"I think they all would," Bridget said with a sigh. "These Drexians of ours love being heroes."

"Especially when it involves a battle," Mandy said.

"Does Dorn have to wait until his brother returns to go back to commanding Inferno Force?" Katie asked.

"No." Mandy's cheeks flushed. "He had to…"

Bridget grinned and elbowed the woman. "Get her knocked up first."

"Oh." Katie's cheeks burned. "They're not kidding about this mating thing, then."

"Actually," Mandy said, her eyes shifting from Katie to Bridget. "I wasn't going to tell you until after the…"

Bridget gave a small whoop and threw her arms around Mandy. "You're pregnant! I knew it!"

"Are you?" Katie asked, as Bridget hugged her friend tighter, then pulled back and touched her nonexistent belly.

Mandy smiled and her entire face lit up. "We confirmed it this morning. Dorn's pretty excited, even though now he's talking about staying here longer than he planned."

"That's great," Bridget said, "I know you don't want him to leave, anyway."

"I still think it will be fun to go with him as he commands Inferno

Force," Mandy said. "But I guess I probably shouldn't do that while I'm pregnant."

"First Trista's news and now this," Bridget said. "Talk about a day of surprises."

"What's Trista's news?" Katie asked.

"Didn't you hear?" Mandy practically bounced on the balls of her feet. "Her mate is on his way to the station. He'll be here in a matter of days."

"And Trista's only thrown up twice since she heard," Bridget said out of the corner of her mouth.

A sharp rap at the door was followed by Reina's blue hair poking into the room. "What's going on in here?"

Mandy waved her in. "What's it look like?"

Reina blinked at the sight of Katie in a wedding dress and her mouth fell open. "I thought I was coming for a party."

"It's called a surprise wedding." Mandy put a finger to her lips. "Once all the guests arrive, Katie and Zayn will walk out and announce that it's actually their wedding."

Reina's mouth had not closed as she gaped at the three women. "Does Serge know?"

Mandy rolled her eyes and put her hands on her hips. "Serge will get over it. All the wedding planning was getting to be overwhelming for Katie and Zayn, especially after everything they went through. When Katie told me the wedding planning was stressing her out, I suggested she do what celebrities do and have a surprise wedding."

"I wish I'd done that," Bridget said. "As beautiful as our wedding was, having to plan it almost drove me crazy."

"I thought all human females loved wedding planning," Reina said looking from woman to woman. "That's why we assign every tribute bride a wedding planner and a liaison. That's why we have dress designers, florists, cake bakers, and even famous musicians appear on the station."

"I think most women do want a fancy wedding," Katie said. "I'm just not one of them."

Reina's eyes darted back toward the door. "Well, I'm not going to be the one to tell Serge."

Bridget touched a finger to the side of her nose. "Not it."

"Fine." Mandy threw her hands in the air. "I'll do it."

"What exactly is this?" Serge's voice carried into the bathroom from the suite. "I hope you people don't think I was born yesterday. What kind of party has chairs set up in rows? Are we watching a movie?"

"You're up," Bridget said, pushing Mandy toward the door.

Mandy caught Reina by the hand and tugged her along beside her. "Then you're coming with me."

Katie watched as Mandy and Reina disappeared out into the suite. She could hear the sound of voices as guests were arriving. They hadn't invited many people, because they didn't know many people. Aside from the aliens on the station she'd met during the planning process— Serge, Reina, Monti, Randi, Sid—they'd only invited a handful of tribute brides and Drexians.

Zayn had arranged for the captain of the space station to marry them, so she knew he would be there. Mandy had arranged for additional canvas folding chairs to be delivered to the suite, and they'd set them up facing the balcony. She and Zayn would say their vows overlooking the holographic African savannah where they'd first met. Katie couldn't think of a more perfect setting.

"Hey." Trista's blonde head appeared in the crack in the doorway. "I've got something for you."

Katie waved her forward. "Come on in. We were just talking about you."

"Why would you be talking about me on Katie's wedding day?" Trista's cheeks turned pink as she entered the bathroom.

Bridget mimed zipping up her lips and Katie followed her lead, not mentioning Trista's mate, even though she had a lot of questions. Luckily, Trista produced a bouquet from behind her back, and Katie gasped with delight. It was nothing more than a cluster of white orchids tied with a sheer ribbon, but Katie's eyes misted over as she looked at it.

"It's perfect." She took the bouquet and gave her fellow tribute bride a one-armed hug.

Trista's nervous smile broadened into a real one. "Preston's assistant dropped it off. She said someone called begging for a bouquet."

"That would be me," Bridget said, raising her hand. "I also invited Preston to sweeten the deal, so if you see a tall guy with a very bald and very shiny head, don't act surprised."

Katie laughed, looking down at the long draping stems of orchids cascading from her hands. "After all the aliens I've seen on this station, nothing would surprise me."

"You think he'll come?" Trista asked.

Bridget shrugged. "I did tell him he'd get to see Serge potentially pitch a fit. That seemed to convince him."

The sound of throat clearing from the doorway made them all turn to the open gap. "Mind if I see the bride?"

"Speak of the devil," Trista said, as Zayn peeked in.

216

"Normally, I'd say it's bad luck to see the bride before the wedding," Bridget said. "But I think the two of you have already had enough bad luck for a lifetime. You should be pretty safe." She winked at Katie and then left the room, patting Zayn on the arm as she and Trista passed him on the way out.

Zayn stepped inside, and Katie inhaled sharply. He wore the dark dress uniform of the Drexian warriors, with a sash running down one shoulder covered with insignia and metals. She'd never seen him dressed up like this, and the sight made her heart race. What was it about a man in uniform?

"You look beautiful," Zayn said, his gaze taking in every inch of her as he approached.

"Thanks, so do you."

He chuckled. "I think you're the first person who's ever called me beautiful."

Katie put her hands on his broad chest and looked up at him. "Their loss."

He bent and brushed his lips across hers, sending little jolts down her spine. She licked her lips. "How is it you still taste like doughnuts?"

"I made sure doughnuts would be part of the wedding reception," Zayn said. He jerked a thumb toward the open door. "I just snuck one."

"Are you ready to do this?" Katie asked. She still found it amazing that a gorgeous Drexian warrior wanted her as much as he did.

He met her gaze and brushed the loose curl off her forehead. "I've been ready since the first day I laid eyes on you."

Katie's pulse fluttered. Part of her still couldn't believe she'd found happiness with an alien, but another part of her felt like she'd been looking for him her entire life.

"It's a what?" Serge's voice from outside the bathroom rose to the level of a shriek. "But she doesn't have her something blue!"

Zayn rolled his eyes and pulled Katie closer. "Let's go make this official, mate. I'm very much looking forward to the part that comes after this when all the people are gone."

"The honeymoon?" Katie's eyes went to the freestanding bathtub, then to Zayn, and she bit the corner of her bottom lip as he let out a low rumble. "That makes two of us."

Epilogue

The Drexian slammed his fist on the hard surface of the table and peered across the room to the man standing in the shadows. "Will House Baraat ever stop being a thorn in our side?"

The elder Drexian rocked back on his heels. "They may have prevailed this time, but they have no idea about our plan."

"Which is now crippled thanks to Kax and Dorn. Our Kronock friends won't be pleased about this."

"It is not our fault they did not use the advantage we provided them." The older man had thick hair that had gone almost entirely silver, and he dragged a hand through it. "Yes, we'd hoped for a more disabled station, but it was only a matter of time before Zayn's implant was discovered."

"Now what?" the younger Drexian growled. "I'm tired of waiting."

"And I am tired of watching my people defend these inferior humans. We save them from destruction, yet they seem bent on ruining their planet regardless. These are the creatures with which we are supposed to further our species?" The elder's lips curled into a sneer. "I think not. No, the sooner we end this unnatural dependence on Earthlings, the better."

"For the greater good." The younger warrior echoed the words he'd heard so many times. "But what if Kax and Dorn decide to probe further? Can they trace the deception back to us?"

"I am a member of the Drexian High Command and a descendent of one of the most elite families in our empire." He spit the words out. "They cannot touch me." His voice returned to its usual, measured tenor. "Now, I need to attend a committee meeting about our unfortunate security breaches."

The younger Drexian watched him sweep from the room. As much as he revered the old man, he suspected his influence and stature would not save him from charges of treason. No, it was up to *him* to ensure the evidence did not point their way. He thought about some talk he'd heard earlier about an incoming warrior and grinned. He knew the perfect scapegoat.

Preview of Book 4: RANSOMED

Chapter 1

Torven leaned against the weathered bar and eyed the green-skinned Grindul pouring drinks behind it. He'd been to enough seedy outposts to know when his drinks were being watered down. He glanced around the dimly lit room and tried not to inhale the smoke that hung in the air like a thick haze. This place was as seedy as they came.

"Noovian whiskey," he said, holding the alien's gaze. "Straight."

The heavyset bartender grunted, but he seemed to size up Torven's build and the similar bulk of his Drexian shipmate, his eyes flicking to the Inferno Force insignia on their uniforms before nodding. If the Drexian uniform didn't scare people, the flame insignia that represented the warrior race's elite fighting force did. The Drexian Empire may have been known throughout the galaxy as a race of warriors who defended those weaker than themselves, but their elite Inferno Force was the team known for enforcing their might with equal parts justice and fury.

Inferno Force warriors were rough and battle-scarred, and spent most of their time fighting on the outskirts of the galaxy. They weren't a usual sight at this particular trading outpost, but one look at their tattoos and longer hair, and the various aliens in the bar had given them a wide berth.

The bartender poured a generous amount of green liquid into a glass and slid it over to Torven.

"Scaring the locals again?" Torven's best friend asked, as he thumped a hand on his broad back.

Torven picked up his drink and tossed it back in one gulp, feeling the whisky burn on the way down. He turned to Dakar. Even though his friend was tall, as were all Drexians, he still had several inches on him. "No trouble this time, my friend."

Dakar cocked an eyebrow. "You haven't even met her, and you're already on your best behavior. I'm impressed." He eyed Torven's face. "Now, if we could only get you cleaned up a bit."

"There will be time before we arrive on the station." Torven stroked a hand down his stubbly chin and brushed a strand of dark hair off his forehead. "Until then, I want others to know I'm Inferno Force. It keeps the local troublemakers in check."

Dakar's gaze dropped to the thick, black lines under his friend's eyes. "I don't think that's a secret."

Originally worn by Inferno Force before battles, many of the warriors had permanently adopted the markings as a warning to any they encountered. Considering the way creatures in the bar had flinched when the two massive Drexians had entered, it seemed to work.

"You promised no fights during our journey," Dakar reminded him.

"You know I never pick fights. I only right wrongs."

"I know, my friend. There is no more honorable Drexian than

you." Dakar picked up his own glass and swirled the contents. "Your high standards do seem to get us into more than a few fights, though."

Torven raised his empty glass in salute. "The price to pay for doing what's right."

His friend took a long gulp. "Who's going to keep us in check while you're romancing your new bride?"

Torven leaned back against the bar, thinking of the tribute bride he'd be meeting in a few days' time. Even though he'd seen her picture, he knew little about the human female chosen for him. Like almost all Drexians, his name was in a lottery for one of the human brides, since female babies on his world had become a rare occurrence.

Instead of allowing their race to die out when they realized the birthing trend, the Drexians had scoured the universe for compatible species and had happened upon Earth. Even though Earthlings had some physical differences, about half of the females had enough genetic similarities to make them suitable for mating.

After waiting for years, Torven's name had been chosen for the next available human mate. From the image he'd been staring at since he'd gotten the notification, he knew she had pale, wavy hair, and blue eyes. And he knew what he'd already known about all human females—they were small in comparison, and had only two breasts, and no arousal nodes down their spine. What had been a surprise was the jolt of familiarity he'd felt when he'd first seen her face on the screen. He knew it was impossible, but he felt like he already knew this female. Even her image stirred his blood in a way he'd never experienced before.

"I'll be back before you know it," Torven said, tapping the edge of his glass for more whiskey.

Dakar gave a snort of disbelief and ran a hand through his own shaggy, brown hair before pulling it up and fastening it into a knot on the top of his head. "I doubt that. You're lucky, though. I hear they've halted transport of humans until the High Command is sure our enemy won't attack them. They don't want to risk the females."

Torven's temper flared as he thought about the Kronock, the Drexian's sworn enemy, and violent creatures known for invading and wiping out entire species. As a member of Inferno Force, he'd been fighting them on the outskirts for years, holding them back, and protecting the solar system that contained Earth. When the Kronock had attempted to invade Earth over thirty years earlier, the Drexians had stopped them, discovering that humans were compatible with their species in the process. The governments on Earth made a deal with the Drexians—protection from the Kronock in exchange for human mates. It had worked well—the Kronock had been held at bay and Earth had been saved.

However, only recently, his people had discovered that the Kronock had been hiding their technological advancements and were planning a massive invasion of Earth. The recent incursions had been the reason he'd been unable to join his waiting bride until now. He couldn't abandon his shipmates in the middle of a battle. Even now, part of him felt guilty taking leave.

"Maybe I should wait until after we've defeated them once and for all," Torven said. "Inferno Force needs every warrior."

Dakar shook his head. "This war may never end. If you don't claim your bride, someone else will."

Even though he'd never met her, he'd been staring at his mate's image for weeks, and already thought of her as his. The idea of her with another Drexian made him clench his fists.

Dakar laughed. "Don't worry, Torv. As soon as our shuttle is refueled, we'll get out of this dump and head for the station."

Torven slammed back the whiskey the bartender poured him and glanced around the dive bar. He supposed this outpost was as good as any for fuel and supplies, and it was located halfway between his fleet and the space station where he'd meet his bride, but he also knew it attracted smugglers and arms dealers and all sorts of lowlifes. He watched as heads huddled together at the bar and money was passed underneath tables in dark corners. Even the air he breathed was tainted with sour-smelling smoke as patrons used bubbling inhalers to get their high. The sooner they left, the better.

"What about you?" he asked his friend. "You on the list for a bride?"

"I'm on there, somewhere." Dakar shrugged. "I'm a third son, so I won't come up for a while."

Torven nodded. He knew one of the reasons he'd finally been matched was because he was an only son. He would be the only male to carry on his family's name. Although he wasn't a member of the elite class, he was descended from a long line of valiant warriors. It was no secret that brides went first to the elite families, and then to only sons. Third sons like Dakar would be farther down the list.

"You could become a captain and move up the list," Torven said, taking the refilled glass from the bartender. "Our commander didn't even put himself on the list and was called away because he got matched."

Dakar choked on his laughter. "Commander Dorn was practically dragged off his ship. I pity the female who got matched with that battle-hardened warrior."

Torven allowed himself a smile. He, too, remembered the stormy look on their commander's face when he'd had to leave the fleet and report to the Boat, the space station where tribute brides were housed. "It will be good to see him."

Dakar nudged him. "You'll have to tell me all about the Boat. And the fantasy suites."

Torven's face warmed. Even though he'd never seen the space station, the stories about it were legendary. It had been designed with human pleasure in mind, and contained everything human females loved most. He had no idea what those things were, but he knew the station was nothing like the old battle cruiser he'd come from. He only hoped he wasn't a shock to his bride.

He rubbed a hand across the scruff on his cheeks. Warriors in Inferno Force battled in the farthest regions of space, so they were allowed to be rougher around the edges. Torven wondered if he should try to appear less wild for the Earthling, like Dakar had suggested. As he debated the possibility of being clean-shaven for the first time in years, he heard a commotion from the entrance to the bar.

Murmurs passed through the crowd as a group of uniformed Drexians entered—these warriors with close-dropped hair and starched uniforms—and many patrons drifted away, as the heavy boots clomped across the floor. The green-skinned bartender disappeared, as the four warriors approached Dakar and Torven.

Dakar raised an eyebrow and muttered under his breath. "And I thought *we* weren't welcome."

The lead Drexian soldier looked both men up and down when he reached them. "Torven of House Kantar?"

Torven shifted his eyes to his friend before answering. "Yes?"

"Your presence is requested by the High Command."

"I know," Torven said. "We're on our way to the Boat. This is just a quick stop for refueling."

"It's a long trip," Dakar added with a grin.

The other Drexian didn't smile or acknowledge Daker. "You need to come with us."

A suspicious tingle ran down Torven's spine. He'd sent word to the space station that he was en route. Why send a squad to intercept him? They knew he was traveling with Dakar so his friend and crewmate could pilot the shuttle back to Inferno Force. "What's all this about?"

The Drexian crossed his arms in front of his chest. "We are here to bring you in for questioning."

Dakar held up his hands. "Whoa. Questioning for what? This guy's on his way to the Boat to be matched with a tribute bride."

"Not anymore, he's not." The lead Drexian let his eyes slide over to Dakar before returning to Torven. "He's wanted for questioning in a criminal matter."

"A criminal matter?" Torven gave a small shake of his head. "I think you have the wrong Drexian."

"Negative." The warrior clamped an iron cuff around his wrists before Torven could react. "You, Torven of House Kantar, are being charged with treason and conspiring with the enemy."

Torven's mouth dropped open as he stared at the shackles on his hands. He heard his friend protesting loudly in the background, but all he could think about was the pretty blonde who would never be his.

Chapter 2

Trista sighed as she slipped out of the suite, letting the doors slide closed on the loud festivities within, and feeling relieved to be in the relative quiet of the corridor. She could still hear the music pounding and the peals of laughter, but she was glad to be by herself.

"Macarena!" someone screamed from inside, and Trista shook her head. Yep, she'd escaped just in time.

The surprise wedding had evolved from a pretty ceremony over-looking the African savannah (courtesy of alien holographic technology) to a dance party that would probably go until late in the night, if the Palaxian booze had anything to say about it. Her feet, which she'd jammed into high-heeled stripy sandals for the party, already ached.

It wasn't that she didn't enjoy celebrating with the other tribute brides on the space station. All the other Earth women were great, but if she was being honest, Trista felt like she didn't belong.

She glanced down at the simple yellow sundress she had on. She'd much rather be wearing jeans and a loose-fit T-shirt, and the second she got back to her suite, she was losing the dress and heels. Not to mention the makeup the tribute bride liaison, Reina, had put on her. She knew tribute brides were supposed to look a certain way, but when she looked in the mirror and saw her usually wavy blonde hair blown stick straight, and her blue eyes heavily made up, she saw a stranger.

Breathing in the cool night air, Trista stopped along the wooden pathway and looked out over the holographic environment. Even though the savannah was dark, she could hear the sounds of animals and the rustling of tall grass in the breeze. The alien technology that created all of it was pretty amazing, but it was another stark reminder that she was out of her league.

What would the other tribute brides say if they knew what she was really like? They seemed pretty accepting—they'd adapted to living with aliens, after all—but what would they think if they knew about her past? Her new friends on the space station included a former ballerina, an Instagram influencer, and a reporter. That was a far cry from dating members of a motorcycle club and not even holding down a real job, unless you counted working on the broken bikes for no pay.

A bird cawed loudly as it swooped overhead, and Trista jumped. Even though the aliens had cleaned her up pretty well and given her an entirely new wardrobe containing nothing black or leather, she felt like she was living a lie. Not that she wasn't grateful for being rescued from her crappy former life. Being taken from Earth was the best thing that had ever happened to her, especially since she'd been running from a particularly bad ex-boyfriend. She shuddered even thinking about Rick and his nasty temper. No, she was glad to be far away on a space station. She was just tired.

She sighed as she slipped off her shoes and hooked her index finger through the heel straps to carry them. Tired from the party, but also from trying to pretend she belonged, when deep down, she knew she was a complete fraud.

Technically, none of the Earthlings belonged. They'd all been taken from Earth by the Drexians—huge, brawny alien warriors with bronze skin and muscles for days. Guys who would have been way out of her league back on Earth, Trista's little voice reminded her.

The Drexians were smart about taking women, she'd give them that. They only took a few at a time. Plus, the chosen women had to be one-hundred-percent compatible with Drexians—not all were —and have few family and friends to miss them.

"That would be me," Trista muttered to herself, as she padded in her bare feet along the wooden walkway toward the inclinator.

She'd been taken from Earth and brought up to the Boat, the high-tech space station that resided behind Saturn and housed all the tribute brides, as well as other aliens who kept the operation running. That had been a few weeks ago. The other two brides she'd been brought up with, who'd become her friends, were already mated to their guys. She still waited.

If she was being completely honest with herself, Trista hoped her Drexian never arrived. She couldn't bear to see his disappointment when he saw that he'd been matched to someone who wasn't beautiful or hard-bodied or glamorous. She touched a hand to her hair, remembering that her stepfather had always called it dishwater blonde, and made a face. Who wanted that?

Trista could imagine how a big, alpha, Drexian warrior would react if she told him she hated wearing dresses and liked working on engines. The Drexians tried to make all the tribute brides happy, but she doubted they would let her tinker with their spaceships. That would go over like a lead balloon. No, she'd rather stay in her perpetual holding pattern on the station, than have her Drexian realize he'd gotten a D-list bride.

Not that waiting on the Boat was a hardship. The station had been designed for the sole purpose of enticing human women and making the process of being taken from Earth and paired with an alien mate more palatable. The Drexians and the other aliens who had designed the station had taken inspiration from Earth movies and TV, and had even nicknamed the station after the show *The Love Boat*.

Trista laughed to herself as she walked, thinking of the dated television that had inspired the station. The influence of the 70s and 80s could be seen in everything from the decor to the fashion, not that it bothered her much. She reached an arched doorway and swiped her hand across a panel. When the doors swished open, she stepped onto the inclinator—like an elevator that could go sideways as well as up and down—and heard the 80s Muzak piped in overhead.

She hummed along with "Take on Me" as the sleek, white compartment surged up, the uplighting giving the walls a lavender hue. Her suite was only one floor above, on the Greek Isles wing, and as she stepped out of the inclinator, she saw the familiar, whitewashed buildings clinging to the side of the hill that dropped into the sea.

Of course, it wasn't actually a Greek island, but the Drexians had such sophisticated holographic technology that it not only looked like one, it smelled and sounded like one. Trista breathed in the scent of saltwater, and heard the waves slapping the sides of the fishing boats in the harbor.

Each tribute bride was placed in a holographic fantasy suite designed to look like an idyllic setting—from a South Pacific over-water bungalow, to a ski chalet, to a safari suite on the African savannah. Somehow, they'd known that this mix of bright-white houses topped with blue domes, and pink flowers spilling down the mountain, was her dream vacation—a place she'd never imagined she'd ever see when she was stuck back in a small town in the middle of nowhere.

She walked up the wide, whitewashed stairs until she reached another arched doorway, and waved her hand across a flat panel.

"Trista!" the voice from behind made her pause and cringe.

She'd been so close. Turning, she smiled at the tall, willowy woman with light-gray skin, and a shock of blue hair that curled straight up from her head. "Reina, I thought you were still at the party."

"The wedding, you mean," Reina said, giggling. "Can you believe those two managed to plan a surprise wedding that even Serge didn't know about?"

The doors to her suite glided open, and Trista looked longingly inside. "How is Serge? Did he recover from the shock?"

Reina tapped a spindly finger on her chin. "It may take him a while to get over the disappointment of not getting to plan a splashy wedding. He *is* a wedding planner at heart. Luckily, he's got your wedding to distract him."

Trista's stomach did a series of flips at the thought of her wedding. The Drexian warrior she'd been matched with was a part of their elite Inferno Force, and had been delayed battling the enemy on the outskirts of space. "I'd have to have a groom to plan a wedding."

Reina hooked an arm through hers, and walked them both inside the suite. "Like that's stopped Serge before."

Trista knew that was true. The pint-sized wedding planner—from an alien species called Gatazoid—was a force of nature when it came to planning. She'd seen how he'd pulled together weddings for the other tributes, sometimes in a matter of days.

"Have you given any more thought to what you'd like for your wedding?" Reina asked as she crossed the living room, her heels clicking against the polished white floors, and opened the sliding-glass door that led onto a balcony.

Trista sank onto one of the white, slipcovered sofas as her pulse quickened. The last thing she wanted to think about was a wedding, especially since she'd never laid eyes on the man she was supposed to marry. She knew she could opt not to be mated to him, but then she'd have to go live with the few humans who'd rejected their matches on the other side of the station. There was no returning to Earth once you'd been taken.

Part of her thought that she could learn to like anyone, especially since all the Drexians seemed to be gorgeous and built. Another part of her knew that there were some things she could never live with again. Things she'd promised herself she'd never tolerate.

"Trista?" Reina asked. "Your wedding?"

"What? No, I haven't really thought about it," Trista told the Vexling, as she came back inside and took the chair across from her. "I wasn't the type of girl who grew up daydreaming about a fancy wedding."

Reina cocked her head. "I thought all Earth females wanted huge weddings. Don't you all want to 'say yes to the dress?'"

Trista thought about her ex-boyfriend, and how all she'd wanted was to get so far away from him he'd never be able to find her. Her heart raced, and her mouth went dry. Even though she knew now he could never get to her, the fear still clawed at her. She inhaled deeply to steady her breath and managed a smile. "Don't believe everything you see on TV."

"You look a little green, hon," Reina said. "Did you drink too much at the wedding?"

Trista gave an abrupt shake of her head as she pushed bad memories from her mind and took a couple of deep breaths to help her heart rate return to normal. "I'm fine."

Reina stood and crossed to the wooden sideboard against one of the whitewashed cave walls, pouring a glass of water from the carafe. "If we're going to take you dress shopping tomorrow, you need to be feeling your best."

"Dress shopping?" Trista took the glass and gratefully sipped the cool water.

"Regardless of what type of wedding you have, you'll need a dress. Even Katie with her surprise wedding had a dress."

Trista drained the glass and set it on the wooden coffee table. "Dresses don't look good on me."

"What do you mean? If I understand Earth phrases correctly, you have an hourglass figure. You'd look lovely in just about any design."

Trista heard herself repeating phrases her ex-boyfriend had hammered into her psyche. "I've got thighs like tree trunks, and my boobs aren't perky enough."

"Perky enough for what?" Reina eyed her. "Earth trees must be very small, if your legs are the size of their trunks."

"I'm not like the other girls," Trista said, hearing her voice crack.

"No," Reina said. "Your hair is lighter, and your eyes are very blue. Is this not desirable on Earth? I thought men liked yellow hair."

Trista shrugged. "Not my kind of blonde." She waved a hand over her nose. "And I have freckles."

Reina squinted at her. "Those pale dots? Are those not desirable, either?"

"They're not exactly sexy. At least I've never been told they were."

Reina stood and joined her on the couch. "I think someone told you these things, and you chose to believe them." She patted her hand. "You would not have been chosen as a tribute bride if you were not deemed desirable."

"That doesn't mean my Drexian will like them," Trista said, giving voice to her fear.

"I think any Drexian would be pleased to be mated with you." Reina squeezed her hand. "You worry too much. I'm sure once your Drexian warrior arrives, everything will be perfect. You'll see."

Trista let out a long breath. Maybe Reina was right. She needed to stop worrying and leave her past behind her, once and for all. But that was easier said than done.

A pounding on the door made both women turn. Reina hurried over and opened it, letting Serge practically fall into the room.

The small alien wore a mango-orange suit with wide lapels and flared pants, and his matching platform boots gave him the extra inches needed to reach Reina's waist. His purple hair was spiked and flushing pink from the roots as he waved his hands in the air.

"This is a catastrophe," he said, as he began pacing.

"What's happened?" Reina asked. "I thought you were at Katie's wedding."

Serge paused. "You mean the wedding they planned without me? That's a topic for another day, let me tell you." He waved his hands more and resumed pacing. "No, this is about Torven."

"Torven?" Trista repeated the word. "That sounds familiar."

"It should," Serge said. "It's the name of your fiancé."

Reina put a hand to her mouth. "Don't tell me he was killed. I don't know if I can handle another Drexian mate being killed in battle before he reaches the Boat."

"Worse," Serge said, his voice dropping, as if he were afraid of them being overheard.

Trista's stomach clenched, both at the thought of the fiancé she'd never met, and at the prospect that something worse than death had happened. "What could be worse than being killed in battle?"

"For a Drexian warrior, being arrested for treason," Serge said. "He's being brought here to appear before the High Command."

"Treason?" Trista collapsed onto the couch. So much for everything being perfect when her Drexian arrived. "When?"

"Now."

———

To order RANSOMED and keep reading, go to the next page!

About the Author

Tana Stone is the sci-fi romance author of the Tribute Brides of the Drexian Warriors series. Her favorite superhero is Thor (with Jason Momoa's take on Aquaman as a close second), her favorite dessert is key lime pie, and she loves Star Wars and Star Trek equally.

She has one husband, two teenagers, and two neurotic cats. She sometimes wishes she could teleport to a holographic space station.

She loves hearing from readers! Email her any questions or comments at tana@tanastone.com.

f facebook.com/tanastoneauthor

Printed in Great Britain
by Amazon